THE WRECKING BALL

A NOVEL

THE
WRECKING
BALL

CHRISTIANA SPENS

HARPER 🌑 PERENNIAL

NEW YORK • LONDON • TORONTO • SYDNEY • NEW DELHI • AUCKLAND

HARPER ● PERENNIAL

First published in Great Britain in 2008 by Beautiful Books.

P.S.™ is a trademark of HarperCollins Publishers.

FIRST U.S. EDITION

Designed by Phil Mazzone

Library of Congress Cataloging-in-Publication Data

Spens, Christiana.
The wrecking ball : a novel / Christiana Spens.— 1st Harper Perennial ed.
p. cm.
ISBN 978-0-06-164934-9
1. Young adults—Fiction. 2. Self-destructive behavior—Fiction. 3. Psychological fiction. I. Title.
PR6119.P45 2008
823'.92—dc22

2008019489

08 09 10 11 12 OV/RRD 10 9 8 7 6 5 4 3 2 1

For Mariota and Flora

THE WRECKING BALL

Thursday, July 5

ALICE

I don't even want to think about last December in Manhattan so I change the subject and light up a Marlboro and pretend I'm interested in London Fashion Week when truth is I don't give a fuck. Rosé pretends she can understand what I'm saying even though we both know I can't string a sentence together anymore, and I'm not really talking, I'm just regurgitating an article I half read in *Vogue* this morning over my breakfast of orange juice and vodka.

"... And I'm so intrigued by Gucci's new inspiration by the Russian Revolution and the whole Socialite Manifesto is obviously so relevant and yet ironic and yet I'm actually more attracted to Versace ..." I get distracted suddenly by a cute car in the street, we're on Piccadilly and it's little and red and I don't know the make but it's probably an Aston Martin and I gasp and say, "That's adorable," but I fail to put any passion into my exclamation and as I say it realize I sound fucked and decide I'm boring Rosé and she's boring me, and "It's been so great seeing you, but I have to be somewhere, you're looking gorgeous by the way, speak soon yeah?" and cut across the busy street and make my way to the Lansdowne because it's close and I need a break from the city, it's so crowded and I'm sick of having to make such an effort just to walk in a straight line.

Summer's beginning to fade outside and the skyline's drenched in its usual smoggy burnt umber causing me almost to fall into a slumber, only I don't because I have to look something close to socially acceptable.

So I order a vodka cranberry and pick up a *Tatler* and let my mind wander.

And I'm wired and I'm tired as I notice the chair is the color of marijuana and I begin to smell the chair though have a feeling it's only the scent of my jacket, a white Miu Miu thing.

The blandly elegant surroundings make me feel comfortable and soothed and I sit back and sink into familiarity and old glamour. Another text message reminds me that I still have to RSVP to my friend's twenty-first that is tomorrow or the next day, but I'm only going if Harry's going, and as he hasn't called me back I just don't know anymore, and I wish he would call because I want the attention, but sadly he's too high to care. He's a bit of a player, you see.

It's occasions like this, when I'm feeling vapid and forgetting details like the day and the time and the city and the point of it all that I wonder where it all went wrong, knowing that I should have known better, wondering why I didn't . . .

Why now I have to go out sixty nights in a row, trying not to notice that it has started to affect my once fresh image with signs of debauchery and abandon . . . that now people think I'm just another wasted Sloane with too much money, martinis and marijuana. And I can't decide if I care what people think or not.

I'm feeling a bit out of it as all the memories flash by, feeling a sort of rush as the past seeps into present—or maybe it's just the cocaine, I don't know.

Over years of sleepless nights and early mornings I have tried to piece the nights together. I used to check my phone to see which people I called, and found strange new numbers, and strange new names, thinking it was all quite funny. Only I'm not really laughing anymore because the novelty has worn thin, so I just gaze into reminiscence with a rush that isn't really high anymore, just familiar, remembering events forgotten again so many times, all adrift in the bacchanal.

———————

Although Alice grew up in South Kensington, her parents divorced when she was thirteen and her mother, originally from America, put her into boarding school in Connecticut, and things suddenly became all confusing.

She started smoking, fell into a bad crowd of aspiring models and socialites, and drowned her sorrows with raspberry vodka in an Evian bottle during classes. She acquired a Connecticut lilt, a Calvin Klein pout and an athletic boyfriend. By the time Alice was fourteen, she had it all.

By the time she was fifteen, she wanted more.

So that summer she lost her virginity at a party in Long Island to a preppy drug dealer and had an acid trip that changed her life.

In a twilight drenched in humidity, the sky was all one color, all one shade of blue. The buildings were clear and defined and minimal, looking like they could fall and fold back at any moment, just bits of paper. These buildings had self-

destructive inclinations, the houses were made of cards and cars and roads were built up like paper.

"Your innocence is fucked!"

Some of the houses fell apart easily and lay in sheets of color on the ground. All the cars were big. Alice heard the music of two threads and not much more than that. Dan said, more demure now, "This country is fucked." The lights streamed by in lines. The light at the junction shrouded the faces in red light like masks. The car swerved. Even though it was all folded down, the simple silhouettes of buildings were pretty in a bland kind of way, paced out and spaced out and meaningless.

The car stopped sometime. Alice got out and went to get a ride home from Miranda, because her purse was in her car. Alice was sitting next to Jordan again, the skinny girl smoking a cigarette now. They drove off and after ten minutes Alice lit up a clove and smoked out of the open window, looking at her bubblegum pink nails and the golden ash flying out behind. Some ash got into her hair but it didn't seem to matter. The driver seemed not so coherent and for a lot of streets they were lost. Her boyfriend passed out but it was just a joke. Then they started arguing, "Quit yelling, Miranda—I don't know where the fuck we are any more than you do."

The city passed by looking two-dimensional and devoid, dark and minimal and clear. The moon was cut in half, the sky was bubble gum chewed until all the color drained out. The car parked and Alice said thanks and got out, saw the car pull away and disappear into the bland symphony.

Buildings just never quite looked the same after that.

More trips followed—some bad, some good . . . Alice chased the unknown like tonic chases gin and the soul

*yearns for sin, with reckless curiosity in the beginning
and yearning for oblivion and escape as reality got a little
grayer.*

*School finished, then she took a year out, and then one
gap year turned into two gap years turned into three. She
learned how to make sushi, took a professional bartending
course, shot a lion in Kenya and dope in Peru. She spent a
major cut of her trust fund on cocaine, and a major cut of
her time in similarly addictive company.*

*Her boyfriend in her second gap year was a man almost
twice her age but with the developmental age of a nineteen-
year-old. His name was Hugo, another crack baby who
never grew up . . .*

*He went to Charterhouse originally, did no work ever,
but playing hard paid off because he invested his trust fund
in shares in a club and the addictions of Generation Z.
When people asked what he did he said he was in acquisi-
tions. When people asked what he really did he said he
could acquire the best cocaine all pure from his contacts in
Bolivia.*

Alice never thought to ask what Hugo really did.

*He worked in New York, Alice played in New York, so their
relationship worked for a while. But there was a rift of de-
fensive detachment between them that made their affections
for one another rather affected after a time.*

*When they broke up, Alice tried to explain to people
that it was because they both had attention deficit disorder,
which was true, but nobody believed her and thought it was
just a euphemism for mutual adultery.*

*She met her current boyfriend, Harry, a dilettante in an
unsigned rock band, on a flight from New York to London
in the winter. Alice had been in the States for a week but*

couldn't deal with it so took an early flight back. She noticed Harry in the line for the plane, kind of recognized him, and found herself seated next to him by chance.

He was her stranger on a plane. They got drunk together and high on the altitude and some cocaine Harry had smuggled onto the flight, and found out they were a lot like each other, liked each other a lot, and reciprocated the lust each other had for life—and for illegal situations in enclosed spaces.

When they got back to London they kept seeing one another, and it turned out that their mothers had been friends, and Alice and Harry had bullied each other when they were five, though neither of them remembered it very well. As the relationship developed, it turned out that little had changed. If anything, the bullying, and their memories, only got worse.

Alice decided quickly that they were meant to be together. Harry wrote songs about her, which she loved, even if they were mostly about her drink problem and penchant for powder. Her addictions were his addictions. It brought them closer and it tore them apart.

Harry was educated at Harrow, though liked to give the impression he grew up in Hackney, where he just started renting a flat that summer. It was where his late father, Charlie, grew up, and where Harry said he fitted in—though he knew that nobody else could really see it. They didn't particularly care if he fitted in or not, as long as he paid the rent.

It meant a lot to Harry though. Charlie died of a heart attack only a couple years ago, aged forty-nine, suspected to be the result of a twenty-year crack habit and stressful career as one of London's most successful cocaine/art dealers. Harry was oblivious to it all when he was younger, and didn't know anything about him except that he was away on business trips a lot, probably to Colombia, though he never specified and Harry was taught not to ask questions. He didn't know anything until the court case, and by then everyone knew.

Charlie got out of it though, as he always did. His lawyer, Harry's best friend's father, defended him in court and he was never convicted. Charlie died soon after the case closed, however. People whispered that when society failed to send him to prison, God put him there instead. Others implied that someone else, playing God, had put him there. Nothing was certain but the fact that he had died, on a first-class flight to Las Vegas. Sin City was his final destination.

There were other bad rumors circulating polite society at the time, accusing Harry's mother, Kate, of having affairs when they were married, of living off dirty money. Those people hadn't spoken much when Charlie was still alive, mostly because the people who criticized Kate also relied on Charlie's cocaine. So she moved to New York for a year while it all died down.

It was all going on while Harry was still at Harrow, and he told people it was convenient to have a new pad in New York. In truth, he missed his parents. But he had been feeling abandoned since the tender age of eight, when he was first sent off to boarding school, had always felt neglected, and couldn't make sense of anything because he didn't know who his parents were, who they had ever really been, and consequently he didn't know himself very well either.

He was accepted in clubs he grew to despise, and rejected from the only places he really wanted to be. The displacement was enough to send him running to a place he could always go—somewhere in a cloud of smoke, somewhere in an empty bottle, somewhere, he knew as well as any other alcoholic, that would always punish him for his unwaver-ing loyalty to a place he came to think of as his only real home . . . The unreality of a daydream, the lie of a high, the trips of imagination rolled up in a joint.

And that was where Alice wanted to go, with him, rather than alone—which was fine at first. But Harry went astray and called less and less as the months fluttered by. And he started to leave Alice behind, and then she found that she was alone in this place that wasn't really home at all.

ALICE

I try to distract myself and pick up the copy of *Tatler* and turn to the page that has a picture of Harry and I, sip my third vodka cranberry and vaguely notice that it's getting grayer outside, and study the picture and see that we look good together. But I'm strung out and sad and can't tell if this is a moment of clarity or only confusion, when I begin to think that no matter how many parties we're seen at together, nevertheless we are drifting apart, and starting to resemble models in an advertising campaign, in a show of faux seduction.

So I throw down the magazine and sip some vodka cranberry, realizing that eleven a.m. is a bit early to be drinking vodka . . . And partly I can see that Harry is turning into a fraud, and that I am too—that the glamour doesn't really satisfy me at all. Even the most artful propaganda of high society fails to convince me that I'm happy, that there is any meaning to it all. And I want Harry, and entertain the thought that there is meaning in that, that I love him.

But no matter how hard I try to believe that we have a future, I can't, because I'm in love with a fraud. And part of me is beginning to tire of the lies. But I can't take the truth.

So I stand up and walk to the conveniently sign-posted Powder Room, cut a couple lines, and put on mute that voice in my head, let the music play me to a distraction instead.

HARRY

I stretch over to my jacket and find my Marlboro Reds and a lighter and light up and take a drag, the smoke clinging to my dry mouth. I don't feel like being awake particularly.

I check my phone and have twenty-two missed calls, some from my mother, some from Alice. My mother is threatening to send me to rehab. Alice is threatening to join me.

"Harry, it's Alice." She's crying. "I just don't understand why you don't want me. I love you. We've been together for almost six months. You can't just leave me, I need you." Sobs again. "What's wrong with me? If it's the drinking, then I'll go to AA. I just want you. Where *are* you?"

I can't feel anything but aching dispassion as I listen to each of the tedious messages, all in the pained Sloaney whine that is so familiar. It's how my mother sounds.

But I don't want to lose Alice, no matter how irritating and tedious she is. We come from the same rich and scenic background, were brought up going to the same extravagant tea parties and share the same dealer, accountant, and therapist. So when she said we were meant to be together, it seemed to make sense.

• • •

The boutiques of Notting Hill are in pieces as I trip along smoking the fifth joint of the day, and it is a soothing day, and I have never realized Notting Hill is so incredibly beautiful before now.

My phone beeps and partially shatters my dull euphoria. It's my mother. I let it ring, it doesn't seem important, there is so much time, I can just let it flow.

My mother leaves a message, an angry one, which I hear later, asking why I'm never home, asking me what I'm doing about my application for Law at Cambridge, asking me, "Do you know the dangers of dalliance?"

But I don't want to be a lawyer—I want to be a musician. So I'm just waiting for that record deal to happen . . . waiting for something big and exciting to happen.

Only all the big and exciting things that happen to me aren't what I want at all.

And as I pass out next to a vintage clothing boutique, it dawns on me that the record deal will never happen, that Alice will never love me, and that the murderers will find me eventually. And I'm not being paranoid, because I read the stories in the papers.

Leo grabs me as Notting Hill blurs out of sight, hails a cab and drags me in, and takes me back to Hackney.

ALICE

In the Wolseley early in the evening, I'm sitting with Harry and a vodka cranberry at the bar. I like going here—the bartender occasionally gives me doubles at no extra charge, if I look particularly rough. He's Australian and in his thirties, and seems paternal toward me. On this occasion, however, it's Harry who looks rough, and the bartender isn't showing much sympathy.

"Can I see an ID for that, sir?"

Harry looks up with his most jaded expression before pulling out a British passport grudgingly.

I speak softly because we both have hangovers, "You know you really shouldn't carry that around."

"I don't have a driving license yet."

"Not even a provisional?"

"No."

Harry sips merlot with glazed tired eyes.

"I thought they were losers anyway," I say.

Harry doesn't reply.

"You'll find some other band, it can't be that hard."

"Maybe it's just not meant to be," he says.

"What—your career? Your life? Don't be ridiculous."

"I'll do something else. I'll do filmmaking. Or acting."

"But you're a musician."

"Nobody wants to hear it, Alice, nobody cares."

I finish my vodka cranberry and smile at the bartender as he walks by. "Grow up, Harry. It's one setback. You'll find something else."

"I don't know why you think you can control me. You don't even know me."

"If I don't know you it's only because you never call, you never want to speak to me. How can I know you if you won't let me come near you?"

"I do—I do want you."

"You act like you want me, then you leave me again. *You're controlling me,* you're playing games with me. You're playing games against me."

"If I don't want you around it's only because when you're with me you try to control me."

"I'm with you now and I'm not trying to control you. I'm trying to know you. But you won't let me come close."

"You are controlling me. Even though you don't do anything. You haven't got a plan either. You're just expecting to strut around, cocktail in hand, until someone proposes. And you'll be so wasted it won't matter who he is, as long as he can keep paying for your drinks."

"I can buy my own drinks." I'm tense, then I sit back in the leather seat and look at Harry. "And I only want you anyway. And I have a plan. I'm just taking another gap year, then I'll do a fashion diploma, then I'll get a job. I'm just enjoying my youth."

"There's more to life than enjoyment," he says.

"We both know that's not really true."

And the conversation spun 'round like this until the original point was lost.

HARRY

I smile, thinking she's sweet, wishing it were true.

We part ways out on Piccadilly—Alice to some club to use the pool—and I go home. I take the tube to Knightsbridge and walk five minutes to my mother's empty flat, second floor of an old Victorian house, with high ceilings and a musky smell of lilies and furniture polish and old cigarette smoke. I haven't been home in weeks. It isn't really home, but where my mother moved after Manhattan and the resurrection of her reputation. It's an exhibition of her independence.

The flat is very stylish, with paintings and many rows of books, a black wicker chair in one corner and several small sculptures and objects. The light in the room is warm and soft, the deepening dusk outside dense powder blue, grains of dark clouds smeared over the horizon. I sit down on the sofa and look out the window at the city in the distance, noticing how elaborate the buildings are, how decorated with details, and yet so simple.

I flick through her stack of magazines—*Tatler*, *Vogue*, *Harper's*, *Vanity Fair*, a few fashion books, a thick volume on seductive shoes, another called *Rare Birds*.

Rare birds are going extinct.

And I think of Alice, her tiny frame, her flights and fights, and delirious eyes, and wonder when she will leave me.

The sky turns darker still. The buildings outside are harder to see, the details hidden by the night, and I sit back in the sofa, my eyes tiring of prettiness. The lamp beside me picks up dust in the air, floating around sublimely.

I cough, my eyes stinging from all the dust and allure and the smoke of my just lit cigarette. My mother doesn't show. I take a shower, change my clothes, and call some people.

ALICE

I'm swimming slow laps in the pool and gazing around at the Art Deco surroundings. In the pool everything seems to slow down and clarify or blur, depending on how I look at it. I dive into the water, touch the bottom of the pool with my fingers, and shoot back up again. I breathe, wipe my eyes, look around, and then submerge again to swim to the other end and climb out. Then I do it over again. Sometimes I swim around for longer, thinking and not thinking, depending on the night, and sometimes I lie floating on the water's surface looking up into the night's sky and its moon, dust and stars accumulated.

After my swim, I'm all set for another traipse around London's habitual masquerade. It never really changes. You can change your mask and be someone else, but the setup is always the same.

Tonight I'm close to Harry. Although we're meant to be seducing each other, somehow it matters that we have an audience. The more jaded we become, the more exhibitionist, the more dazzling the show, with powder and pills exaggerating the effect somewhere in between Fabric and Cuckoo. We're another Power Couple (or Powder Couple).

This cocaine confidence, I wear it so well.

The power is sucked into the toxic atmosphere and we become it and it becomes us, turning into little soldiers on marching powder, defending the euphoria and prepared to lie for it, prepared to die for it. Sort of conscripted by the guest lists to a war against ourselves—friendly fire.

As we're taking the cab to the Cuckoo Club, Harry asks Leo:

"Where's Patrick?"

"He's coming later. He had to go to AA apparently."

"Since when has Patrick been so American?"

"Since his girlfriend left him."

"Sad."

"Ya."

Leo rarely smiles extravagantly, he keeps his poker face intact as the stakes and company get higher, but has a tender look about him, eyes that girls drown in regularly. His father is a top defense barrister, his mother a Parisian actress—so he knows how to intimidate when he so desires. Only the whole thing seems to bore him. Maybe not, maybe he's only acting bored . . . maybe it's thrilling him—or maybe it's killing him. It's always hard to tell. Whatever his demeanor, he's wearing it well.

He retains an air of charm that silences those who would otherwise question his elusive character. People distrust and trust him for the same reason: he has lips that would never tell. And sustenance for my habit.

I trip as I step out of the cab and already I'm in my own little world of hearts and diamonds. Harry catches me and

I kiss him, and we walk into the Cuckoo Club . . . A mass of people, worshipping the same trappings of liberty, and I still can't decide if I like it or not, being captivated by music that uses drugs as another instrument, as an amplifier, air-brushing everything, making sweaty people look attractive and lights shoot diamonds of glamour. And suddenly I'm nervous and shaky until someone passes me a drink and says, "Drink this," which I do, standing closer to Harry, who is distracted by someone else.

"I'll be back soon, I need to find Leo, wait here."

He leaves me and I drift toward a small door that looks too small to walk through, but it's okay because the closer I get, the bigger it gets, and I'm able to walk in and stand in the queue for what seems like hours and hours, especially as a girl in front of me is wearing a watch that keeps ticking, which I realize is strange, because *nobody wears watches anymore* . . . and yet, it keeps ticking. *Tick, tick, tick, tick, tick, tick, tick, tick* . . .

HARRY

Patrick calls Leo while we are still in Cuckoo and tells him we should meet them at a house in Belgravia, where we've been invited to another party. Eventually I find Alice laughing to herself in a corner. She's looking beautiful and wasted, such a pretty stoner, wearing a black mini with sheer tights and black stilettos, her hair disheveled, eyes defined with black liner, her skin glowing with the radiance of youth and adrenaline and her eyes yearning for just a little more of that. She's not really looking at me. So I put my arm around her and lead her outside.

We take a cab with Leo to Chelsea, and Patrick meets us in the street and takes us up. Alice knows one of the girls, Marina, and they air-kiss, which I find so irritating, and as I'm making a drink I hear them talk about a mutual friend, Zara, who was apparently in rehab, though rumor had it that she was actually getting cosmetic surgery of some kind and rehab was only a cover-up. "Being mentally unbalanced is way more chic than being physically imperfect," says Alice. And she should know.

Patrick has scored some intense acid, says a man called Jack, who looks too old to be at the party, at least thirty, but is in fact only twenty-two. Marina is speaking loudly and telling Alice and really the entire room that, "He's a typical example of London Face. It's when, if you live in London too long, your skin ages prematurely, from all the smog. It's called London Face." The fact that Jack can hear them doesn't seem to matter.

"Hey maybe that's what Zara was getting fixed," says Alice.

I turn to Patrick and light a Marlboro Red and block out Alice's voice and fall into a captivating conversation with Patrick about the afterlife and I'm asking, "What if it's just one long bad trip? You know the kind where you feel like your hands are on fire?" but then distantly hear my name mentioned, specifically my father's name mentioned, by Alice, so I move toward her and ask her, "What are you talking about?" She doesn't respond, just stares past me in a trance. "Alice?"

Marina speaks in a faint whisper, "I thought your dad was dead."

"He is . . . What the fuck are you on?"

"He's there."

And I follow the entranced gaze of Marina and Alice and feel a blow to the head as my father—pale, gray and strung out all miserable—looks at me urgently and then disappears, shutting the door behind him . . . shading the soundscape with echoes and the air with dust . . .

Come closer . . .

I stumble as I push my way toward the door.

"Where is he?"

Nobody answers, just looks at the ground or the ceiling or the door, wherever their thoughts have taken them, in a Wonderland of their own making and breaking. I rush out into the corridor and see an open window, the rose silk curtain billowing soft in the dry breeze, and run toward it, only to be mesmerized by the glittering city in my sight, shooting stars and purple clouds of smog, and no trace of my father but a residual cloud of dirty smoke.

Friday, July 6

ROSE

I'm recovering from a tedious night and having flashbacks, and especially keep remembering how some guy in Crazy Larry's, I think, kept following me, and I kept moving somewhere else, and he kept following me, and then I got paranoid because all the guys there looked the same, wearing the same preppy shirt and blond hair and high eyes . . . Eventually I ended up just pushing him away and getting a drink from the bar as Martina disappeared with some Italian and Lola disappeared into a bathroom stall and an ecstasy all of her own.

At that point I received a call from Alice, who said she was in some place in Belgravia and that Harry's father had come back from the dead, at which point I assumed she was on acid or whatever and tried to comfort her, saying, "It's only the drugs, Alice, it's only drugs," which didn't really filter through. "No, this is real," she said, "I always thought it was only drugs, but now Harry believes me too."

The line broke up and I couldn't hear her very well

anyway so I went outside and took the call there, pausing for a cigarette with the other smokers and waifs. I said to Alice, "I didn't realize I was a smoker until the ban came in, and now I'm sure I smoke more anyway," and she replied, "Like a year ago I had no addictions. Now if I go a day without pills or cigarettes or a vodka and cranberry I'll just fall into a deep depression, which is so tedious, you know?"

I knew. It was a sobering thought—and I didn't like being sober.

"Are you really okay, Alice?"

"Yeah, I'm fine, I think I need a cigarette too . . ."

"You going outside?"

"No, it's someone's house, they don't care."

"Okay."

"Yeah I'll see you Sunday, ok? It's been too long."

"Okay, see you then—lots of love."

"Bye."

I threw my cigarette into the road and walked back inside into the sweaty crush and went back to the bar because I didn't know where else to go, couldn't see Martina or Lola anywhere, they were off getting laid or getting high. I knocked back another vodka Diet Coke and talked to some Irish student and found his voice seductive and was talking to him about the Strokes when Martina arrived with a postorgasmic radiance and snatched me away. The Italian was smoldering in the distance and I thought he looked a bit sleazy but she was under the impression he was something special, probably the vodka talking, but maybe I'm wrong.

Then I began to fade and just wanted to leave, feeling nauseous to my soul, wanting someone to hold me but seeing nothing but preppy boys in pastel and toxic eyes.

• • •

The hangover and the morning come and go. The tunes I dreamt linger on.

I play some summer lullaby over and over again, and don't tire of it at all. I could probably survive happily with just coffee, cigarettes and pills. And my guitar . . . I play a simple melody, remembering previous nights: the serotonin-starved pretty people, an addictive decadence woven into strung-up melodies . . .

A duel with a glow stick . . .

Lyrics as colorful and jaded as a sunset viewed through dark glasses and glazed eyes . . .

More hotel daydreams—these strands, these songs, as I put the guitar down and lie back on the bed in temporary accommodation watching the fan whir, and sun daze light over sparkling dust strewn lightly through the air, all hot and dry this July afternoon.

I get up and go to the bathroom and splash cold water over my face then go back into my room, I'm only wearing a little sundress but it's still too hot. I put some music on . . . I listen to the Foals, remembering a gig some time ago, almost a year . . . I listen to "Castles Made of Sand" by Hendrix . . . and some song by the Books, something by Air, breathing some smoggy London version, reaching for the chardonnay, feeling displaced but it doesn't seem to matter because it's a sensation that has become habitual and I have begun to like it—one more acquired taste, one more new combination, one more variation.

I've been Alice's best friend since we were three years old and subsequently we were sort of sisters. We fought all the time, we shared clothes and confessions, and went out to pretentious bars and cafés with one another. We looked like opposites but attracted people when we went out together because we complemented each other. I was brunette and nineteen, deliriously inclined and insecure, but with the pills to deal with it. And I had Alice, who prescribed her own medications.

We have been detached from one another in recent years, since Alice was living in America and I was at a comprehensive in London. We wrote to each other during that time, but it was really only in the past few months that we have rekindled our companionship and realized a mutual tendency for the same vices and highballs and lowlives . . . Even as Alice has strayed into vacuous socialite circles and I am in love with a grungier bohemia, we are still connected by a stronger bond.

As children we were friends because we went to the same prep school and our mothers took us to the same picnics on Hampstead Heath in the summertime. Harry was there too, chasing girls from a young age. I chased boys likewise. He was like a twin to me, looked pretty similar and sulked with a comparable pout.

Now we drink cider there instead of apple juice, and talk of how so much has happened so quickly, how surreal it all is, how hungover we feel, smelling of stale hash and wearing bruises and cigarette burns as accessories that happen to also reveal debauched nights out and misadventures so hard to remember.

We both had better memories of each other before the blur. And when it all gets to be too much all over again, when Alice can't remember who she is, and I can't remember where I'm meant to be going, we go back to before the blur, and somehow those flashbacks trace us back to the starting point, to the center, from which we have so deliriously strayed. When we trip over and fall to the ground, and can't get up, sometimes it takes memories of the baby steps to remind us how to walk again.

•   •   •

I learned to walk in Paris. I also learned to smoke there, and drink there, and pull boys under the moonlight there.

One twilit June I gazed out the window of a plane and saw big bad London turn miniscule as the I lifted higher into the gray smog, which looked quite pretty up close.

I was staying on an edge of the Seine. My aunt put me in a room annexed to her apartment, in the old servants' quarters, where light beamed through two small arched windows, and the ceiling slanted to reveal a view of rooftops and the steep walls down to the street below.

Some yellow roses stood in a vase on the chest of drawers in my room, between the two arched windows, and the edges of petals picked up light from either side. The window on the left had a tendency to open spontaneously in the night and sent a cool breeze into the room. Beams of blue light from the Tour Eiffel cast over the dark sky slowly, picking up light clouds. In the daytime, the light shone rays into the room so that the walls were bright and illuminated, and I was deliriously happy because I was free in Paris and out of the net of neurosis and sadness back home. I could think at last. Only I didn't especially want to.

So I put off thinking for a while and drew roses in the Marais, the noon sunlight on the steps light and dusty. The trees in the courtyard arched over and spread dry green leaves, the coffee and gelato gave the air sweet artifice and the neon crêperie sign was lit in a dim red and glowed. Light glistened in people's eyes, spread shadows over boulevards and red haze reflections blinded me to any dirt there may have been. It only glittered in the sun.

That afternoon I drank mint tea in a flower shop in the Marais with a twenty-year-old musician who played me a Beatles song on his guitar. I had been sitting outside in the street drinking fruit juice and looking around and he was reading a script on a wooden chair outside the flower shop because it was sunny and bright. He beckoned me in with pretty eyes.

His English wasn't very good, and my French was forgotten on account of perhaps something in the mint tea, so we communicated with smiles and songs. I found it sort of ridiculous but sweet all the same. Such encounters weren't du jour.

He was an actor preparing for an audition for the role of Charlie Chaplin in a show to start in August. He didn't look at all like Charlie Chaplin, but had light brown curly hair and bright brown eyes, such an innocent, sunny disposition, it was refreshing. The flower shop was cool and dim inside. There were lots of people in the street outside wandering around in groups and pairs. There were large dark green plants with straining branches and large shiny green leaves falling low on the ground. The floor was tiled black and white and in the window there were reflections of vases and pots and petals as the people moved by outside. I watched them from a chair behind the desk at the back of the room. The mint tea was very sweet and a euphoric perfume hung in the cool but humid air.

He poured more mint tea from a small metal teapot that looked old and slightly dented but very shiny, and we talked *in fragmented phrases about flowers and songs, and I was bemused by the situation, feeling like a romantic innocent, if only for half an hour.*

Later, as the gold seeped down invisible into the indigo midsummer night, bright lights illuminated the mechanical lace of the Tour Eiffel. The crimson streams of lights from cars invited me into all the traffic and blur of the crowd, the people pushing over the streets as waves in an ocean sweeping over Paris. I absorbed the crimson air and neon lights diffused in the delicate humidity.

The neon lights of ice cream vans and the carousel were more luminous and defined against the still deepening sky. Statues of men on horses stood by carousel horses, antiquity and present galloping as one, Paris dancing. The traffic was frantic and the people lit up, lights merged and played in the infinite darkness. It was especially radiant around midnight, and groups were scattered over moonlit steps and the grass by the fountains and shone in gold with the statues, framed by columns and windows.

I lay down on the grass and saw all the pretty stars, thinking that they looked the same in London, unwittingly missing what I had tried to escape, realizing dreamily that I just left behind the only people I really wanted to be with. All the people in the crowds only illuminated their absence. It was not the city, the setting, that mattered—I wasn't running away from London. I was running away, once again, from the confrontations I feared and desired, and in so doing ran away from myself. I was running in the same circles, putting on the same show as everyone else. And I couldn't stop. I was running away from where I belonged, and the friends I wanted to be with. Only wherever I went, whether in person they were present or not, my friends were absent-

minded, and I was losing them, and whether in Paris or London or sober or drunk I couldn't get back what I lost, what we lost.

So the beat went on and on—different paces affecting residual chaos—and I was aware of all the people, the anonymous crowd in which I was lost, the deep red reflections on the marble, and gold blocks of light dividing buildings into lines, defined by darkness to the shape of a stage, and people sitting around casually smoking, talking, singing, eating, drinking. I pushed through the crowd down the steps and walked past the fountains, groups of students on the grass, air full of traffic and crowded lights, the traffic of the stage, onto which I had wandered.

And I couldn't see the road for the cars. Couldn't see the dark for the stars.

It all got so messy after Paris.

ALICE

I'm sipping a glass of light white wine in the Armani café in Knightsbridge with Rosé. Unfortunately, I'm still slightly hungover from the previous night, when I drank too much in No. 5. Harry flaked out on me last minute for no reason, so I followed friends, one of whom had a boyfriend who was an actor who had a membership there. I watched the others dance with all the sex appeal of mannequins in the club as I downed numerous vodka cranberries and elaborate cocktails and faded into the atmosphere, watching the crowd of media people and socialites dazed by a hard day's play.

Time passed fast. I saw the sunrise, something I usually avoid. There was a sense of melancholia that shadowed the day's pale horizon.

I slept until twelve, then awoke to meet Rosé as I had promised.

When we meet, she is looking all excited and neat, mainly because Cambridge starts the beginning of October, where she's going to study social anthropology. I always forget what that means, and Rosé always reminds me:

"It's the study of human civilization. Or lack of it. Speaking of which, how was Natalia last night?"

"The same. She's modeling now. Had to leave early to catch a flight to Fiji for a photo shoot."

"And she's not even pretty. Just plain."

"I know. Such injustice in the world. Did I tell you about my traipse round the agencies last week?"

"No."

"Well needless to say they don't want me. ICM said I wasn't their type. Storm said I'm too short. By an inch. I might go on a protein diet to get taller. It's still possible—my grandmother grew an inch when she was twenty."

"But are you really too short?"

"Yes, I'm five feet seven. I have to be five feet eight. Stupid rule."

"But Kate Moss is five feet six."

"Yes but Kate Moss is Kate Moss."

Rosé is drinking a latte. She looks at me with a sympathetic expression that makes it look like she cares, though I suspect she doesn't care at all, but then maybe I'm being a bitch, I don't know . . . and she says,

"Just keep trying, you're beautiful."

It's always good to get some affection, though, even if it's a lie, and I smile modestly and reply, "Thank you. Only it's not getting me as far as I had hoped. Hollywood gave me false expectations of life."

Rosé pauses, then says with bright, if pretty dilated, eyes, "You know you'd make a brilliant actress."

"Really?"

She nods enthusiastically. "You look like Keira Knightley. But blonde."

"I don't. But that is so sweet, thank you!"

In the radiance of each other's lies, we prance around the Armani store looking at sultry Italian leathers and shoes that scream bondage, and silk waistcoats for women. "I want, I want, I want," we sigh, making mental notes, showing off, getting bored. "Let's go."

ROSE

I drift and browse through Vivienne Westwood's collection with Alice at my side, picking out the armor, the trappings of amore—makeup and make-believe painted prettily on the face of adversity, mannequins bearing punkish attire. Whether in high society or low society, subversion is the fun to be had. The same glare and the same pout . . . models look bored to death.

The fox fur and chains of generations, strung up prettily.

Alice flashes a self-affirming glance to the mirror.

I look away, out the window, and notice the bland shade of gray the sky insists on wearing. The big smoke it exhales and blows in my face.

As the years roll by . . . Decadence and decay are never out of vogue.

● ● ●

Around eight I get a call from my friend Ben, inviting me to a little gathering in his flat in Bethnal Green, so I leave Alice and go meet him.

I take the Central Line out east, feeling a bit faint already from the gin and cigarettes and maybe because I haven't eaten anything but crisps today. I meet Ben at the tube station and hug him and notice he's gaunt and the track marks like graffiti on his pale skin. We walk awhile to his flat but the party is over because of the police or something so we follow everyone back via tube to someone else's flat in Kentish Town. Inside there are paintings stacked against the wall and it turns out that the flat belongs to an artist who apparently exhibits the endless gallery of hallucinatory moments his imagination has spurred in the depths of night.

"I'm just trying to realistically portray the fourth dimension, but people keep describing me as another Postmodernist Abstract fucker, and I'm like, *Nah man, I'm keeping it real man, this is Realism yeah?* But they just laugh at me and give me more coke and tell me to have another couple canvases done by October."

We drink and smoke and I talk to this guy who's in a jazz band and then a music journo who's telling me about how much he fucking despises the Kooks and all the commercialized shit they represent, and then I try to light a scented candle but accidentally set my nail on fire.

ALICE

After Rosé abandons me to chase boys in bands in Camden, I go with Hugo to Nobu Berkeley: handsome man, cute venue, and he leads me by the hand with all his languorous charm and careless generosity. Technically he's my ex-boyfriend but really he's a great friend and all I've got right now, the only one who gets all this because like he says he's been there before.

We eat incredible sushi and drink hot sake and talk about life and love and failed relationships under the elaborate silver leaves of the chandelier, the circled tables of advertising people contributing a buzz and a flow and careless glamour, all mellow like the glow of a dying match head.

The wine bottles glint in the racks—green, blue, pale, high ceilings, high clients, high society, and I can't help but remember meeting Harry up high in the sky and tell Hugo so, and tell him more than perhaps I should, but he doesn't seem to mind. He says he knows what I mean. (Though I don't understand what I mean.)

And of course it's ridiculous that I should have so much baggage when I'm so young—but I'm too jet-set for my own good and I don't travel light.

HUGO

Alice is sipping sake and I'm pretending to care about how she feels abandoned and she misses America and hates her parents and all the rest of it. I'm considering slipping some Rohypnol into her water or the sake when she makes her next trip to the loo which I'm guessing will be about five minutes, because either she's vain and needs to check her reflection a lot, or because she has a little habit going on, or because she is a girl and wants to phone another girl and compare boys and sushi restaurants or whatever it is girls talk about.

I realize it's slightly inappropriate to try and drug and sleep with Alice when we're not officially together anymore, and people will think it's suspicious if she passes out too soon. But I can't be arsed waiting for her to fall for me again. And realistically no one's going to remember anything in the morning. No one ever does.

ROSE

I must have passed out sometime after the flame licking my scarlet nail was extinguished and I wake up when the room is slightly emptier, with someone's jacket over me in a corner. I've woken because an irritating little dog that someone was feeding coke to is licking my face, but I just push it away and go back to sleep to the soundtrack of someone playing "Set Me Free" by the Kinks on his guitar. Early in the morning the dog wakes me again and since nearly everyone has gone I decide to leave as well. The artist says good-bye and I say thanks for the jacket and "Your paintings are awesome," and leave.

I get back home at six thirty a.m. and sleep some more, dreaming I'm flying in a plane where clouds and mirages float by and the lightning shakes us with turbulence.

The flight is mostly vacant and I lie down and fall asleep, then wake again, look out the window and notice that the clouds are the color of pink champagne. The air hostess brings me a coffee, some grapefruit and a croissant. I listen to an acoustic version of some Kinks tune as the plane lands, and I wake up, surprised to find that this time a coked-up dog is not licking my face, and there's no more music, only the gray silence of an overcast Sunday morning.

ALICE

I wake up in Hugo's guest bedroom but can't remember anything of the past twelve hours, only a strange feeling of miserable déjà vu and assume I must have blacked out, which was dumb. I'm aching and feel miserable and want to go home but not really. I want to go somewhere.

I can't think straight as per usual. I look at the painting on the wall, which is a montage of different pieces of trash painted to look appealing. I feel I've seen it somewhere before. Reminds me of Mahiki and Crystal and Boujis and my best friends who never even phone, how they glitter like old metal. The artist is some man named Tobias, neatly written in the bottom right corner, and I want him to paint me. If he can make an old Coke can look sexy he could make me look decent.

HUGO

Wake up and sniff coke.

I go into the guestroom where Alice is sitting up in bed and tell her she passed out in a cocktail bar on Berkeley Square and that I took her home and looked after her because you know I'm sweet like that. She laughs and then she cries because she has a headache so I suggest we go out and get coffee somewhere, and she agrees.

She's always so distant though, and when we're walking through the streets of Kensington she's elsewhere, and I wonder if she remembers anything about last night. Until she starts crying again and hugs me and says she wishes Harry was more like me because I'm the only one who isn't just selfish. It's a gray morning and I want her gone. I take her to a coffee shop, buy her a latte and then leave with a smile and a lie about going to help out a friend when really I'm going back home to get some sleep as I have been wide awake all night and for days and nights and days and nights before and my entire life has become shaded by the twilight zone.

Red lights and the girls outlined by scarlet silhouettes are telling me to drive faster, their faces blinded by headlights—an oblivion made of white light, a morning made of night.

ROSE

Hyde Park, a little high:
Eyes to the sky, bare feet in the grass, and strung-out strumming of guitar—nothing to do but lie around and dream of festivals and a summer of love not so far away . . . not too far gone?

In the chorus of the song I can hear the leaves rustle in a breeze, the clouds drift, time has flickered away with the tune, like a gentle candle burning down slow. And all that is left is pictures in my mind—of people and open spaces, songs that silence the restless crowds or rouse them higher.

The lingering happiness of summertime . . . secret gigs in the woods . . . the bright-eyed independence of rapturous dancers . . .

I'm lying on my back in a field with a slumbering crowd, another summer's day in Hyde Park, some kind of pastoral scene in the middle of the city.

I chase the pills with a song, clamber into the lifeboat of a tune, its beat is ceaseless as the oars of a boat beating the ocean and a shovel cutting into the soil of a cemetery. The voice keeps digging at melancholy like the gravedigger . . .

Despair is buried with a tune—bad memories and serotonin smothered by dust and medications . . .

Each fragmented thought made into a chord or a phrase, then a song, collected together until a record is made . . .

Avoiding the draw of soulless shortcuts, bad music . . .

Escaping the vacuum of diluted styles and sounds . . .

Lyrics are carved into violin like a silhouette etched into copper . . .

Distill the sound, distill the spirit,
And drink.

Locked in a vault of sensations,

Lost in a labyrinth of lyrics . . .

Euphoria is cut up like cake or coke into a careful rhyme scheme . . .

We're distracted to ruin.

HARRY

There are so many realities and they are all exclusive to their eyes, people's eyes.

One reality is more . . . than another . . . heavy skies and the way objects fall, the shade of blue and foam, the hurricane, the people who run and those who drown, the expressions on their faces, the music playing—the clocks ticking—the roar of surf and thunder—the last flicker of electricity—fire and smoke, words choked by trouble breathing, skies red with paint, nerves controlled by powder, nights in lights guiding traffic down a stairway to heaven.

The law doesn't like people to see this colored smoky volatile certainty because they are scared of their own incomprehension. I do want to see. Intoxication is illegal but I am too abandoned to care.

Nonsmokers don't understand eternity anyway.

ALICE

I feel such a desire to free my mind.
Though I feel I'm only losing it.

I go to Green Park alone in the afternoon and smoke a packet of Marlboro Lights and feel quite hollow now that I've slowed down and Hugo has left and Harry won't answer his phone. I'm always racing against myself in an effort to chase him. It can't work out if he's too fast for me or too slow. Somewhere along the line our heartbeats went out of sync and we never see each other anymore, not properly.

I don't know what is wrong but it isn't really him
And it isn't really me,
It's always being watched
It's not being able to see
There's something wrong with it all
There's something wrong with me

ROSE

It's just after seven a.m. and I haven't slept yet after a wired night of taking random pills and night buses everywhere.

Now I'm going back home on the tube, I feel like some coffee and a rest in peace—and when waiting on the platform a couple in front of me have a fight and break up in the space of a few minutes. The girl is in her mid-twenties, French, and very pretty; the man I can't see so well, he has his back to me. But from their argument it's clear that the man is unreasonable, he's criticizing the girl for having too many friends, seems jealous of her—and when he hits her, in public, I feel so sad for her, and so angry at him. The girl has tears in her eyes and walks away quickly, and the man walks onto the train quickly, and as usual, everyone around acts like nothing has happened. And I want to say something, want to do something, but it all happens so fast, and I just watch the girl wipe tears from her eyes and walk down the platform alone. And then I'm just miserable again and

I wonder why and remember I forgot to take my Lexapro yesterday and chase one with some Evian pronto.

•   •   •

I sleep a bit in the morning and then wake up with a bad hangover but have things to do so I get up regardless. At one I go to Foyle's Café for a coffee and meet a personal trainer called Peter. He's very good-looking—dark hair, blue eyes, very fit. He comes across a bit nervous-neurotic though, but gives me his card and says to call him. He scores out his email address on the card but I can see through the ink and look it up on the internet when I get home, and it seems he's created this website charity thing all about supporting fathers in parenthood. And I can't think of any other reason for this than the possibility that he himself has kids, which means he's probably in his thirties or something and had a previous marriage (which is a lot of baggage). So we'll see.

I get changed and go to meet Alex in Soho. I go into Umbaba first for the Miss London Party. It's all a bit strange. In the loos I get talking to a Russian glamour model with platinum hair and a snake tattoo on her left shoulder. "Yes, I was very young when I got that, very stupid when I got that." Didn't look that bad actually.

I go back into the club and buy a drink and then randomly meet two boys—a Cambridge graduate and a Bristol graduate and we talk for a while and sip overly expensive vodka and strain to hear one another because the music is so loud. Why is the music so loud? Because nobody has anything to say for themselves, only money to throw at each other. I'd rather chat over cheap gin personally.

Alex is a bit late and by the time he is in Soho I'm so bored of Umbaba and say we should find somewhere else.

He asks why I got bored and I try to express just how tedious Eurotrash socialites are, how creepy the big group of Arabian bachelors are and how annoying overly loud house music can get.

So we go to an Italian bar instead and I listen to Alex's new songs that he has been recording that day with Matt, and drink a vodka cranberry and sip a little of Alex's cocktail, something with espresso. After that we go and find a little blues and rock joint, St. Mauritz, and go down into the basement, a cluster of little rooms with people dancing to old music. I meet some twenty-three-year-old called Dan who is wearing a stripy T-shirt and has lovely eyes and wavy brown hair and for some reason I decide he is beautiful and then go upstairs and outside and kiss him, as we are sitting on the street smoking. Later I go back into the bar and Alex can tell what has happened and thinks it's a bit random. It is. Inside I have another drink with Alex and then lose Dan for a bit, and at three a.m. we decide to leave, since we both have work the next day. We walk back upstairs onto the street and say good-bye to the others that we have met, and I kiss Dan and then Alex and I leave, and then I get the night bus home. When I wake up later that morning I really don't want to face consciousness at all.

ALICE

So I arranged to meet my father for breakfast at the Cinnamon Club. The uppers don't make it any easier. The speed doesn't make it go faster.

Daddy runs a PR company and hardly sees me, and I feel abandoned enough to look for love in all the wrong places, though he gives me a pretty generous trust fund to make up for it. He's late, I'm sitting alone at a table for two, sipping some coffee and being bored and playing with a twenty-pound note, rolling it up and tempted to cut to the bathroom but don't because I'm high enough already and trying to practice some self-restraint for a change.

I like to try everything once.

I'm remembering school in Connecticut and half wanting to go back to America. Harry mentioned that he was thinking about moving there to further his music career. So I've been fantasizing about moving there with him . . . Manhattan was always my kind of place. I was never intimidated by the city, only in love, another London, only better designed. It was so easy to get around. So I did get around, and then my escapades became my past, and my past became my escape from the present, as I reminisce about a time not so long ago but somehow separated by a gulf of more recent descent.

Manhattan, June 2006
The Beautiful and the Damned Party

ALICE

I sat in bed in an apartment on Broadway, gazing calmly at the screen of windows in front. I paused, felt a kind of destiny in the soft June breeze that disturbed nothing but wisps of curls and movement of chiffon—just a Manhattan sigh.

"I'm leaving in two days. But I'll be back," I said.

"Oh I know you'll be back, it's clear," said a stranger on a park bench.

I wondered how I would get back, smoked a little weed and walked downtown, past Gatsby's Bar and Lounge, past mannequins in the windows and neon distracting the stars with a cosmopolitan glow and burn. I walked fast and in sync with the movement as if a single fish in a shoal in the waves amidst all the seaweed . . .

I walked all the way up to 82nd from 19th because I felt like the walk, though realized that flat shoes may have

been a good idea around 42nd. Nevertheless, I kept walking through the light rain and hoped it would end soon. I
bought some cherry cloves from a cigar shop and the man
behind the counter told me that it's bad to smoke.

"Oh I don't really smoke, I just go through temporary
addictions where I chain-smoke for one night and then don't
smoke anything for months after."

"That's good—I only smoke cigars. Every morning I go
outside, and a group of people are all puffing away. And then
I go out at lunch and the same people are puffing away"—he
mimicked desperate inhalation—"and then I go out at four
and the same group are smoking away again. And I wonder,
when do they ever work? All they do is smoke . . ."

"Maybe they're advertising your shop?" I replied, and
paid for the cherry cloves, he smiled, I walked outside into
the rain and lights sparkling wet.

When it got heavier, I bought an umbrella for a dollar
and walked a few blocks up to St. James's Church, where
a tall serene-looking black man beckoned me in. I went in
and said thank you, and walked down the aisle, kneeled and
crossed myself at the altar and sat down. Another man was
sweeping the altar, its gold and marble magnificence.

The wet umbrella dripped rain onto the marble as I
looked around at the paintings and light brushed delicate
and beaming into the substance of the walls and building. It was as if the man was sweeping the sins caught in
shadows away under a brushstroke, just as the painters
had turned gray stone to celestial light with some pigment
and white.

I could hear no traffic at all in the church and it was serenely
quiet, seemed an incongruity in the midst of Manhattan.

Outside the cars were flaring by in speed and noise, people
hurrying and damp. I felt strange not to be in the church, to

step from celestial to secular in a minute, my own thoughts turning awry with the onset of rain and wind brushing me downtown it seemed, and against my stride.

I went to an Upper East Side salon to retrieve a so-called spa day that I whimsically bought from an actor in the street. I had my nails painted scarlet by a girl called Maria who told me that if I wanted employment in New York City I would have to get highlights in my hair—"You have to have a more aggressive hair color—this color—it is too innocent." The idea of aggressive hair did not really appeal to me however, and the next lady I encountered told me that she loved my natural color and never to color it, but some highlights would still be a good idea. She whispered in my ear in a thick Brazilian accent, "I give you full head of highlights for sixty dollars, not ninety dollars. That a thirty-dollar reduction. And you will get a job."

"But I don't want a job."

I got a haircut and a neck massage and liked the nails, and walked out of the salon. The sun failed to shine and I was not highlighted in any sense, just kept walking, walking, walking downtown past the bland streets of the Upper East Side and smelling food I couldn't eat.

Later, for the Beautiful and Damned party, I dressed in a vintage black dress from Paris, which had a layer of black tulle that skimmed my knees and was tied like a corset at the back with black ribbon. It was pretty and simple and I wore it with a small white leather handbag and high black shoes and scarlet lipstick. I curled my hair like a flapper, because it was a thirties theme, and wore pearls.

I took a cab to the party on Fifth and 42nd. It occurred to me that perhaps it was a stupid idea to come to this party alone, but it just happened that way when all the tickets sold out before I had secured two more for Lara and Jessica, but had already paid up for my own. I had the ticket, so decided to go anyway—why not?

I went up the little steps and some girl checked my name on the list—I left my jacket in the cloakroom and went into the room where the party was. There were not that many people yet so I sipped some white wine, noticed the décor and then talked to a man in real estate for a while. He was fun to talk to, but I wanted more people to turn up soon. Empty rooms always make me feel nervous.

When I went outside to smoke a cherry clove I met an investment banker called Peter and we exchanged life stories and flames and noticed it was not raining anymore, which was such a relief, because for the past couple days June's sky had been so dull.

Now the sky was pink in its benefit party revelry and women in feathers and couture drifted around with men in tuxedos. "So, this is New York. How do you like it?" I smiled in reply, because I wasn't so new to the city as he imagined, because I liked the glamour, l'amour, some—more—felt it oh so natural.

"I'm just slightly miserable because I have to leave in two days, that's all," I said.

"You'll be back, I can tell," he reassured, "you got that drive."

That Manhattan Drive.

He could probably see that I was escaping from somewhere, therefore. Looking for something. He was from London, too. I wasn't sure where I was from anymore.

One reason why I liked Manhattan was because I always met men there who distracted me from school, from home . . . Peter seemed laid back, which comforted me. I couldn't stand stressful people, I liked people who were serene. Consequently, all my boyfriends had been stoners. But now school was over and I began to think that maybe things would change, maybe these men were different.

I was usually too young for them. So we would talk of the island together, flirt with the idea that I might live there soon, when I was older than eighteen, and then you never know what might happen on that fringe of ingenuity on an edge of the island.

• • •

"So, are you waiting for someone?" asked Hugo.

Yes, no . . .

"I just came by myself. My friends couldn't get tickets in the end, but I wanted to come anyway, so I did."

"That's very bold."

I smiled at the man. He had a kind expression . . . It was all so much revelry.

"You want a cherry clove?"

He seemed to say no.

"I mean I don't even smoke," I said, "I just like the smell."

"You gotta be careful."

"I know, my mother says there's a fine line between being a dilettante and an addict."

Hugo smoked a little, so did I, then he threw it into the street, and I followed, like it was a dart, the sparks flying out over the dark pavement.

I remembered when I hit a bull's-eye the first time I played darts, my first term at boarding school in Connecticut, when some older boy was teaching me and telling me he was looking forward to college because then he could just sleep around and be free.

I was bored of school at the time.

The next dart was a disaster and hit somewhere close to the ceiling.

● ● ●

The room was filled with pink light and a dance floor, two bars, feathers, tuxedos, and minute by minute the room began to resemble an aviary of these white feathers and dresses that shone for men who coordinated and reacted as magpies do. I noticed an au fait manner to movements and an idle adult wistfulness as the evening waltzed on, more people—fashion editors, agents, businessmen—joined, met, danced, parted—though the music was nowhere near jazz, but dance music of the modern age.

I was sure that Gatsby was there somewhere—he just wasn't making an appearance. I felt rather put out.

The party featured an open bar and, because I was predictably devastated that I couldn't find a Fitzgerald, the love of my life, or any champagne for that matter, I took the opportunity to drink cocktails indiscriminately.

I could not find a modern Fitzgerald, but it was the Beautiful and Damned party after all . . . white wine, a vodka martini, then a Manhattan, another martini . . . a cosmopolitan . . . another . . . Jack Daniel's was waiting.

● ● ●

"You ever been with an older man?"

It was some not especially desirable lawyer talking to me

over the hors d'oeuvres, so brash. So I said, "Well he was twenty-two." I wondered why it hadn't worked out. The night hung on this thought.

I stopped reminiscing and turned back to the man who was old enough to be my father. He disgusted me. There was closure to flirtation.

I picked up wine from the bar, then talked to some man from Tunisia, I couldn't even remember where Tunisia was, who flew back once or twice every week.

"Don't you get tired?" I asked.

"Yes, but I'm used to it now."

I lost the lawyer somewhere in all the pink light and people. I liked his jacket.

I thought about how I had been flying around so much recently, something I didn't plan but just happened, went outside, sat on the steps, saw Manhattan—it was once a promise of escape, now it was a consolatory presence like the company of a friend I didn't see often enough. I ordered another Manhattan.

• • •

The Creep from Geneva took a light—my lighter had little love hearts printed on the plastic—and insisted on talking to me for some time outside, giving me life advice.

"You have to be careful with men. Men are as opportunistic as women," he said, apparently not trying to be funny. The Creep from Geneva told a story about a woman he knew who pretended to fall in love with an American man with the sole intention of obtaining a green card through marriage. "That's so immoral, I'd never do that, as much as I'd love to live in New York, but there are other ways," I said.

The Creep from Geneva talked about his secluded hotel in Bali and I was getting bored already, then unprovoked he offered me a job and a visa to wherever I wanted to go and then hit on me in a matter of seconds, at which point I smiled with averted eyes and swiftly moved back inside to where other people were, my nice new friends the investment bankers. Hugo and I had agreed to check with one another if either of us found someone especially interesting.

"Did you find anyone then?" I asked Hugo.

"No. I met one woman but . . . ." No words followed.

"And you?" he asked.

"Oh, some guy offered me a job and a visa then hit on me."

"Yeah, you have to watch out for them."

We both looked mildly disillusioned, slightly provocative . . .

"Well it's appropriate, isn't it," I said. "We're at the Beautiful and Damned party, so we're damned not to have a date."

"I couldn't find anyone else because I was looking for you. Take my number, I've got to leave now, but call me."

I took Hugo's number and then he left me.

●   ●   ●

I didn't dance, I didn't especially feel like it. I enjoyed myself though, flitting around in the twilit June, flying casually with the breaths and whispers of the breeze and glitterati conversations, through pink skies that smelled of cologne and perfumes and cocktails. It was relaxed, I drank some more, and interesting, and quietly magical, though I surprised myself in finding it so soft and natural, as if I had traced this all before. I was surprised that I didn't have to make an effort to soar through the sky as the sun set and the moon was waxing.

I was content as I was when I was four years old, curious and active, though without having to think much about it. I could concentrate intently but it didn't tire me, there seemed no struggle anymore. I was caught up in the music and smiles and dusky lights of brief encounters, conversations, walking, turning, moving, yearning, but with a complete lack of desperation. So satisfied of curiosity, even desire was softened with chiffon. My mind was synchronized with the music that played, the beat was mine as well.

It was not so much that I had no desperation, only that desperation referred to the future, and I was not thinking about the future right then.

I spent the end of the night with an actor-musician called Alex. We met at the bar with Jack Daniel's and Jack White playing the guitar.

"I've been at a girls' society school in Connecticut," I said in reply to something like Where Have You Been All My Life.

The man smiled sardonically.

"And what do they teach at those places?"

"They teach girls how to be more confident than perhaps they should be."

"I'm leaving then."

"No," I smiled, "I was a bad student . . ."

I liked his smile. The White Stripes were playing.

The night passed subtly past midnight as we were in conversation. I didn't remember everything people said, it all sparkled effortlessly, and they began to go. I didn't want to be the last to leave the party so I said good-bye to some people, picked up my jacket, and Alex gave me a pink rose.

We shared a taxi down to 19th and we hugged good-bye and he walked off downtown. I took the elevator up to the seventh floor and let myself in, put the pink rose in a glass of water, took off my shoes and dress and climbed into bed, happy, mildly fatigued, content. The moon and a grid of New York lights glowed through the window behind a pink rose, blurring as I fell asleep.

• • •

In Washington Square, daytime sun was shining and I was trying to write letters and postcards to friends, but there were all these people around distracting me . . .

A poseur avec Marlboros, flip-flops, green khaki, aviators, shaved head, gray ribbed tank, exclaiming—"That guy is so cute," he said, referring to similar-looking guy in shorts and shirt with a book. "That guy, is oh my God, SO cute." Hot sky, red toenails, green and white stripes of vending people.

Trees, bricks, a girl drawing cartoons or a film storyboard with long brown hair and opalescent skin, long legs, short shorts. Another girl sat down by the guy with the shaved head: wearing a head scarf, ripped jeans, green khaki jacket, eating a salad hummus pita while talking in breathy monotones to the man:

"Kee-ah's boyfriend is still in my house. She's gone. Actually no, he left for LA."

"She's so adorable," he said without expression.

"She left actually. But I know, isn't she? She's so refreshing. I saw this surf film. I never thought about it, that you can surf in New York. And now, I want to. It's like incredible."

The girl with the head scarf got a sheet of tracing paper

from her canvas khaki tote and started tracing a picture of some trash bags. Another man walked by, he was wearing a T-shirt that read "Brooklyn Tech." Headphones, shades, tans, paper, cell phones, lunch.

She picked up her cell: "Speak louder? . . . How embarrassing . . . Okay, Diego, okay . . . Okay, I'm on . . . Wow . . . Okay, I will keep smoking that . . . I'll send you a new one, next hour . . ." Throughout the conversation she spoke very loudly so that much of Washington Square could hear—the man with the shaved head kept getting embarrassed and muttering, "Ok, yeah, yeah, speak louder? Can you Speak any Louder?"

"Oh my God, that was . . . I wrote 2005 not 2006, I forgot what year it is, and Diego said, Yeah, like keep smoking whatever you're smoking. And I'm like, yeah, I will keep smoking that. So like, I have to get a new one done in an hour. That dog is so cute."

I felt relatively sane and clear-minded after that.

● ● ●

That night, I took the subway down to Spring Street and walked east to Crash Mansion, where Alex's band was playing.

I passed through into the bar, met Alex within a minute and we talked briefly. I sat down on a black leather seat and watched the band playing first, who were a little too anarchic, sipped some vodka on rocks and noticed how well dressed and attractive everyone was, tall, lit, serene in the dark room. It seemed unnatural that nobody was smoking, due to the ban, but I adjusted quickly and the lines and silhouettes were better defined minus clouds of tobacco. I began to think I even liked the clarity.

I sat and watched and then met a student from Cooper Union called Mike with black glasses and dark hair, who told me that he wanted to move to Japan someday but of course loved New York eternally. We talked for some time and then moved closer to the stage to watch Alex's band play. We stood and listened, the band played very well, the bassist looked fun, I liked being there. I wanted to come back, though I only really thought momentarily because I was leaving the next day and didn't know when I was returning.

At the end I ran to quickly say good-bye to Alex before I traipsed into the night with Mike and his friends, but I tripped on the stage and hurt my shin, though nobody noticed apart from the bassist, a blonde girl with a nice smile, who mimed she wouldn't tell. I smiled, hugged Alex and kissed him good-bye, said I loved the music, that I'd be back someday. I stepped carefully down from the stage into the dark room and noticed that my leg was bleeding and swelled up, very painful, but Mike assured me that the fall was graceful enough that it didn't matter.

I walked around the Lower East Side with Mike and his friends and talked about SoHo and music and art. We talked about Ground Zero, walked and walked some more. Mike told me that he had just started school at Cooper Union when the attack happened. He and the other new students watched as all the people ran uptown through the East Village getting away from it all, in dust and dazed, as downtown the skyline disintegrated. "I don't think I ever really recovered from it."

I cried when my plane ascended in the morning, leaving New York all cast in a subtle blue hue was just too sad. I noticed that my leg exhibited a bruise the shape of Manhattan now, the Bowery Bruise, and a smaller one the shape of

Liberty Island. So I had something to take back with me, therefore—New York had branded me. It was a sweet good-bye, but it hurt.

———————

"Alice, what's wrong?"

My father sits down at the table—I hadn't noticed his entrance.

"Oh I'm fine, it's nothing . . . How are you?"

"Fine, sorry I'm late, the traffic."

"Yeah, it's fine." I avert my eyes, because it isn't really fine. I'm not happy. My father is oblivious as usual. I feel bad for him. He's so clueless that he doesn't know or understand why his daughter doesn't love him. I want to love him, but I can't. There is something missing.

He's missing: just never really there. Perhaps I'm never all there either.

But I'm not going to say anything confrontational today or any day. I'll do what I always do—answer him politely and try to be the daughter he wants me to be. I know I don't really match the bland ideal, there's too much turmoil burning me up for that—but I can easily act like a sweet little girl.

I'm humoring him, because the whole situation is too far gone for anything to change now.

"What are you going to have, Alice?"

"Another coffee, please."

"You have to eat, darling."

"Ok."

I pause, glancing over the menu, looking to see what's high in protein and low in carbs:

"I think I'll have the smoked salmon and scrambled eggs please, but without the eggs."

"Great."

He orders a boiled egg, toast and cappuccino.

"So how *are* you? How have you *been*?"

"Oh, just fine. I've been making some gap year plans."

"Great."

"I'm considering a wine appreciation course. I'm interested in the wine trade, and possibly opening a bar when I'm older."

"Oh excellent."

"Ya, because it will be a good development from the bartending course I took in February."

"Of course."

"And since I know so many people, if I opened a bar, they'd all come to it all the time."

"Yes. Well that sounds constructive, Alice, but what about your career in fashion?"

"I can do both. I'll just see how it all plays out."

"Best way, best way."

"I mean, so far, the modeling agencies don't want yet another English Rose on the books. Apparently the Slavic look is more Now, or something. They want Russian orphans but not English aristocratic waifs."

"Oh how awful."

"I know."

"Speaking of orphans, your mother told me that you were in *Tatler* with Harry Law. I don't like him. I don't want you to see him."

"Harry's not a bad influence, Daddy."

"Yes, he is."

No, he's just a boy.

I don't reply to Daddy. The waiter brings the food, I don't touch it.

After the pause, in which Daddy cracks open his boiled egg, he picks up the conversation.

"Alice, being seen with Harry Law will do nothing for your reputation or your sanity. He's dirt."

I know this isn't really true. He just doesn't want me to be happy. Dirt is only another word for dust, for glitter, for glamour, for snow. Daddy knows that.

"Don't be photographed with him again."

"Yes, Daddy."

"He's not safe. Am I making myself clear? Don't play with matches, or the photographs will burn, and your reputation will be dust."

"Yes, Daddy."

Daddy clearly needs therapy. His lack of balance unbalances me.

"Hugo Kent, however, is a different matter. He's one of us. And he doesn't just sit on his arse all day getting wasted."

"How do you know Harry gets wasted? He writes songs. He writes me songs."

"That's very sweet, but he's still wasted. I care, I do."

I look down at my untouched breakfast. It makes me feel nauseous.

"Go out with Hugo by all means. Be seen with him. But not Harry Law."

"Yes, Daddy."

I wonder if he gives this same advice to the clients of his PR firm. Judging from the papers, they don't take his advice either.

"And don't smoke. It's disgusting."

"Yes, Daddy."

• • •

After breakfast, I chain-smoke as I walk to some little bar in Mayfair. I order a double vodka martini and then another and then another, and by eleven a.m. I'm in my own little blur. I try to call people but no one picks up, or their phones are off, or they're engaged. I try calling Rosé a few times, to say sorry for being a bitch, but can't get through. I try Harry's phone again and again but he doesn't pick up. I haven't seen him since Thursday night—now it's Monday and I miss him. I was going to leave a message but am having trouble speaking, so I don't bother.

HARRY

I'm in a pub just off Soho Square, drinking some cider and watching the news on a screen. It's around one and there are all these businesspeople, wearing black and white, some stale tobacco smoke hangs in drifts from the doorway. It's demure inside, dark and relaxing and quiet, and on the screen there's a picture of an alleged murderer. I watch the blank young face of the defendant, looking for something that would betray some humanity, seeing only an impatient disposition, detached from the situation, on trial for murder. His childish eyes are glazing over. It was a revenge crime apparently, over some money. If the prosecution are correct in their facts, it was a completely disproportionate reaction. It was rash, it was pointless, it was quick.

And as I'm sitting here listlessly thinking things over and trying to make sense of things that are senseless, I can't help but think that it could happen to any of my friends—they could so easily be victims or defendants, take revenge, be a subject of it—given a London Baptism one way or another.

Larry, a witness in the trial portrayed in a pastel drawing on-screen, catches my attention when he describes the scene of the crime. A young man, allegedly the defendant, chased a man in his early twenties across the grass outside a bar, and stabbed him to death. Larry was in his car, approaching traffic lights but stationary because of all the people and traffic. There were around a hundred people in the area, from the nightclub.

"Girls were smiling. To be honest, that was what shocked me the most—the coolness of the people around me. Nobody was overly concerned about what was happening around them."

And I wonder if I would have done anything either, wonder if I care enough. I used to think so, but it's getting harder to act every day. It's all performance and no action. I'd like to care but I don't.

No I'm lying again. I'd like to be carefree but I'm not.

• • •

I wake late afternoon from another dream about my father, having fallen asleep on a park bench in Soho Square.

My father was standing in a big room, talking to people, and I couldn't get his attention. I started crying but nobody could hear me. I started flying but nobody could see me, so I flew out the window and flew to the ocean, where I dived in and swam to LA. I walked out onto the beach, climbed over some railings, hailed a cab and went to Soho House, where I drank some absinthe with Courtney Love.

I woke up feeling tired, confused, and rather well traveled. I was sad the dream ended when it did.

Blowing more smoke into the smog of the city, I walk with a lax stride through central London. I'm off to meet my mother for an early dinner. I don't want to see her, but have a feeling she'll cut my allowance if I don't make the effort.

I meet her at L'Etranger on Gloucester Road. I'm late, and she seems quite nervous and shaky when I arrive. She's in her early forties and has recently dyed her hair blonde, in reaction to a few gray hairs and a conviction to have a new life. Her hair is shoulder-length, honey-colored, and her skin is pale and powdered. She wears a dusky pink lipstick and a cream-colored two-piece.

I kiss her cheek and sit down, smelling alcohol mixed with her perfume and realizing immediately that she is pretty high as usual.

"Darling, darling! It's so lovely to *see* you again! I've missed you, darling, you're never at home, never, and I've missed you *so so so* much!"

"I missed you too."

I say it trying not to feel it.

"We should do this more often, shouldn't we?"

"What? Speak to each other?"

"Yes, and spend time together, lots of time. And there's so much time in the day and in the week and in life that there's so much time that we should spend more time—together."

"I think I'll have a glass of red wine. And the steak. Thanks."

"Yes, food. Not especially hungry actually. A salad, please. Thank you. Very good."

I look around the restaurant, mostly boring media types.

"So how's school, Harry?"

"I finished over two years ago."

"No, no, I mean university."

"I haven't applied yet."

"But you got into Oxford, Harry, and I'm so proud of you," she gushes.

"I gave up the place, remember? You already know, I gave it up, to focus on my career in music."

"Don't be silly, darling."

"I'm not. I'm thinking about moving to New York. The music over there is more where I'm at right now. I don't feel comfortable in the London music scene."

"No, darling, I'd never see you. Don't go to New York. I lived there for a year, why didn't you come then?"

"Because, as you know, I was at Harrow."

"Well Manhattan is a long way away. I'd miss you."

"You didn't miss me much when you lived there. And you left me here alone."

"I did miss you, that was why I came back."

"No it wasn't. You came back because Manhattan got bored of you, but London never tires of a fraud."

She downs the last of her red wine. "Don't speak to me like that, Harry. You have no right."

"I have every right. Dad died and you left, because your image was more important than me."

"That's ridiculous."

"And it's true. You found a doctor you liked in Manhattan and a social life you liked so you chose it instead of me."

"What doctor?"

"I don't know, it doesn't matter. You probably can't remember his name because you're so spaced out on the pills he gave you."

"You're not making any sense, Harry, I don't understand what you're saying."

"Because you're high again."

"I think you're high, Harry, I think you need to get some professional help."

"Fuck you." And I knock the red wine over the table as I leave, getting out into the street, humid and dry and asphyxiating.

I take the tube to Camden because it seems far away from Mayfair and walk out of the station to the first pub I can see, the World's End, where I drink gin and tonics, knocking each one down like dominoes, no effort or will required.

ALICE

Ipop a Vicodin and then call Hugo, who has left several messages in the past couple days that I didn't reply to immediately. But since Harry's been so mean lately I'm beginning to disregard him, lose sight of what I guess I thought was love, and look for distraction elsewhere. And I know it's deluded, but I can't resist remembering a rose-tinted past with Hugo and how sweet he was, taking me to Nobu and not pushing relationship questions, just letting me be. It wasn't even that awkward.

I'm anticipating him, imagining him as someone I always wanted him to be, but had never been. Maybe he's grown up a bit now, I begin to think, and maybe he will look after me in ways Harry apparently can't. But it's only the Vicodin sweeping this delusion over a sadder reality.

At thirty-nine, even a stint in rehab to deal with his tragic childhood and cocaine habit weren't enough to push him into psychological maturity. He was still in denial. As he told me once:

"Look, I don't have any issues with cocaine. I have issues with life. I don't like it. It's not fast enough. It should be faster. If life was faster, then obviously I wouldn't need cocaine."

"If life was faster, you would die sooner," I replied, wondering if that was why we all succumbed, so easily, wondering whether death was seducing me, too.

He looked at me with those defiant, sad eyes of his:

"Well obviously it's not a scenario that's really worrying me, is it? It's not a thought that's killing me."

"Actually, it is."

(And can I have some more?)

———————

In a coffee shop one spring day in New York, I met an NYPD detective who gave me advice on rent and life in New York City. I asked him if I could leave my laptop with him as I bought a coffee—not realizing he was a cop. When I returned he said, "You're lucky I'm a cop, 'cause you can't trust no one in this city. Don't do it again."

He was nice, he smiled, he was looking out for me and I could tell he was genuine because he was so fatigued as he said it, like it was his duty—and yet he had a kind expression and voice. He was in his late thirties and had become tired of the city and his job—"I investigate internal corruption. Once they have ya, they've got ya for the next two years, I can't get out of it now. I'm thinking of moving to Florida after that. I've been in this city a long time now."

He said that he didn't like Brooklyn much, with a weary sigh, that no, it would not be a good idea to find a cheap place on the fringe of Harlem—"You're so white, you'd stick out, they'd have ya," and maybe it would just be a good idea to move to Jersey.

"I guess I could be a nanny," I said, trying to think of a way to move to New York, because my father wouldn't agree to support me there, and the detective agreed, and then added on a second thought, "Or you could just move in with a rich man on the Upper East Side."

That was the law and order of New York City.

"Alice, it's so great to hear from you, I've been worrying about you," says Hugo.

"You missed me then?"

"Course. Always. Listen, what plans do you have for to-night?"

"I haven't decided yet. I'm so in demand, you know."

"Well let's talk over dinner."

"That's such a nice idea, only I don't feel like eating."

"A drink then?"

"Perfect. Where shall I meet you?"

"Come to Sketch at ten, on Conduit Street, near Bond . . ."

"I know where Sketch is, Hugo," I say in an insolent tone, then, sweeter, "I can't wait."

"Great."

"Bye."

HUGO

Alice is late, but I don't really care. I expect it. The time flutters by for us both.

I used to like dating Alice because she was so flaky and unfocused and it made me feel better about myself—more mature, more punctual. I liked the feeling of control. And I liked to be teased by her insolence. Our relationship lasted six months on these terms, until Alice just left me without explanation, when we were both in Manhattan, just packed up and left one day and only told me two weeks later. She never fully explained, just said she needed to be alone and it wasn't working and the usual vague things, but then she's young so I let it go, and it was convenient anyway because I was attracted to another woman at the time, a domineering lawyer in her late thirties. Then I spiraled into excess yet again, this time in Ibiza over the summer months. There I discovered that everyone else on the island was at least fifteen years younger than me and I wound up in rehab for the end of summer with the anxiety disorder and consequent breakdown that it caused.

I came back to London feeling refreshed and with new prowess, feeling younger after the detox and with a fresh-out-of-rehab altruism that was as fleeting as the drugs but never mind.

I had a new self-awareness, and a desire to find a younger girlfriend again, who by contrast would make me feel more mature and adult—but not too adult. I admit it, I never want to leave my prime. I don't want to stop. I want to go back to last summer. I don't want to turn forty. I don't think I ever truly accepted *thirty*.

I tried to hit on numerous young socialites, but didn't get very far because they were more interested in young millionaires than older ones and a lot of girls are actually quite difficult to drug. At that point, I remembered how much fun Alice had been, and called her up. I was sure it was only a matter of time before she succumbed to me. But I'm rather impatient so took her out to Nobu that night and made her mine yet again. She is my favorite acquisition. And she doesn't even know it.

ALICE

Hugo, it's been forever—how are you?"

We embrace, he kisses me. I notice he has some gray hair and London Face. I still feel a kind of tenderness for him. His visage betrays a tired man. His voice intends something else.

"Great, really great actually. Amazing summer."

"Really? Where did you go?" I'm starting to feel a strange sense of déjà vu—but I'm sure we didn't talk about his vacation last time we met . . .

"Ibiza. It was amazing. Sun, sex, stimulants . . . All I needed, all on one island."

"I can imagine."

"I bet you can," he says in a sardonic tone he thinks is sexy. "You should have been there."

I smile. "I've been so busy. And London was its own little island this summer."

"Gets awfully humid, though."

"I don't mind it. I've been away every summer since I can remember. I wanted to stay home this year."

"Was it worth it then?"

I think about it, try to articulate:

"Well even by the end of June, London didn't feel like home anymore . . . I didn't go to Ibiza . . . I just . . . brought Ibiza to London. You don't really need to leave the city to . . ."

"Leave the city?"

"You know what I mean though? There are just so many ways of getting away. So many ways to fly away . . ."

"Alice, you told me you were going to clean up your act."

"And yet you love me to play dirty, don't you?"

Hugo smiles. I'm attracted, but don't care enough to make the effort. It just feels good to talk to someone older. I feel relaxed with him. I can say almost anything I want and he'll still want me, because his ideal of me is so deviant that no amount of insolence and angst will deter him. In fact, it would bring him closer.

But I don't want to be intimate particularly. I want him closer, but not too close.

"I'm all right, though." I sip some cosmopolitan and he looks all moody. "I've developed a high resistance to alcohol."

"It's not really the alcohol that I'm worried about."

"What's scaring you so much then?" I ask.

"That you're getting too hard-core for your own good. You don't want to be a slave to any addictions, Alice."

"Why? Because then I can't be a slave to you?"

He looks almost hurt, which is touching.

"You were never my slave. I cared about you. Still do."

"I was only teasing."

"When you told me you cared about me too?"

I smile. He's so easy to tease. Too easy.

"I can't remember."

"You're wasted, Alice."

"It's all relative. I only just turned twenty, there's time yet for me to clean up my act if I so desire."

"But you don't desire it. You desire Harry Law. And you're wasted on him."

"Where do you get this from?"

"I have my sources."

"You've been stalking me? That's so immature, Hugo."

"I care about you, Alice, that's all. I care about you a lot more than that little trustafarian cunt."

"Just because he's got a trust fund doesn't actually mean he's a bad person. I have a trust fund. You never held it against me."

"I like to keep an open mind."

"But not with Harry."

"No. He's bad for you."

"No worse than you. You're more similar than you realize."

"I can look after you, he can't. I care about you. He's just using you."

"You're using me, Hugo."

"You were so sweet at the Beautiful and Damned party. When did you get so insolent?"

"Probably when I started dating you. You know you're not such a great role model yourself. You tell me to sit pretty, but you go to Ibiza to act like you're twenty-two. It's so hypocritical."

"Cocaine doesn't do much for your manners."

"I didn't take any today actually."

"Well maybe it should stay that way. It's not doing you any favors."

"Listen to your own advice. You've got a smear of powder on your shirt collar."

"Least it's not lipstick."

I finish my cosmopolitan, looking at him more tenderly. I love to hate him so. And yet he's so unbearably clichéd and arrogant.

"I should go now. I need to be somewhere."

"Where?"

"Go ask your sources."

Such a stupid thing to say. He brings out the worst in me. I start acting like a B-grade noir actress and it kills me. I kiss him on the cheek and walk out, the victory tainted by the residue of affection, a residue of addiction.

As I walk home, I begin to think of Harry again. I miss him more than ever. Whenever I think about Hugo, inevitably I remember how I ran off with Harry and how much more fun he was. We would run around the city and disappear into a mutual oblivion, and although there were downs for every high, nevertheless, I had never been higher than when with him. I take the tube back to South Kensington, ignoring everyone, in a euphoric lust I know is deluded but love all the same.

———

There was one night especially, in February, when Harry and I had recently hooked up and the moon was full and the glasses were fuller and tinted the color of rosé . . . We went to a party at a musician's flat somewhere near Camden. The whole place was full of instruments, so many guitars and amps and drums and keyboards. We went along with some other friends to this flat and drank vodka and smoked a little weed and something like an hour went by where everyone was just talking and strumming tunes on the guitar. The boy in the band of the moment just mixed people drinks and tunes and stood on the sidelines with a quiet charisma.

Meanwhile Harry led me into the music room and we kissed and the rest. Harry sat on a piano stool and played a few notes, then I sat on his lap and let my hair fall down as I kissed him. Then he pushed me onto the floor and we made out for a while, Harry being his usual pushy self and I enjoyed every moment. Then the boy in the band walked in and interrupted and I giggled and Harry acted like nothing had happened and he hadn't just been undressing me, and then when someone else also came in we both got up and got drinks from upstairs and acted nonchalant and mischievous and thirsty. The kitchen emptied after a bit and I sipped on some vodka and Harry played some music. Then we kissed again and made out on the kitchen floor for a while before I said I preferred the music room actually. So I led him that way and he led me astray. Some girl walked in on us at some point but I didn't even notice. Then we went to sleep on the floor side by side for about an hour before the sun woke us up again, and the cold, and I pulled a black jacket over me to keep warm, thinking it was bad how the winter could be so cold, but all I really needed was a man and some leather and the night no longer made me shiver.

———

The streets outside are dark and damp and the stars like shattered glass in the sky. The cold breeze hits me as I walk home.

And I wish I was wearing something warmer, a leather jacket say.

And I wish I had a man, who could love and who could play . . .

I don't want to go home, I want to see Harry. I call him. As usual, it goes straight to voice-mail, so I leave a message:

"Harry, it's Alice. Can you just call me back and tell me straight what it is you want from me? Because I used to think you loved me, but now I'm not so sure you still do. I don't want to leave you. I never want to leave you. But you're never here anymore. Just call me. I love you."

HARRY

I hear the phone but I can't pick up because I'm cutting up another line and going to a place where Alice no longer seems to exist—I just forget. I forget my parents, forget my friends, forget my problems, lose my mind—forget all the hell of every day as I struggle not to succumb yet again to my weakness but can't manage to stop, can't win, swallow my dignity as my veins burn with cocaine lust and the city smolders, my glittering stage, my conquest, my hell.

Tuesday, July 10

ROSE

I lie in bed with a bad headache and recent memories of a dark night and another two-dimensional façade, a metropolis that looked like a sprawling stage set.

I get up and run a bath with Victoria's Secret bath bubbles, then progress to the kitchen, where I make coffee. I had a strange dream where I was in a forest of tangled branches, I was shooting white birds, not caring at all. I sip some coffee and walk back to my room slowly, turn the water off, sip some more coffee.

I lie in the bath and try to think but it is no use because my mind is still dazed with marijuana and the caffeine has not hit yet. I lie around for quite a long time thinking superficially of all clubs in London I have been to or heard about or want to go to, and remembering the previous night.

I dress and see a blue bruise on my left foot from where a girl in stilettos stood on me. It was a silver stiletto.

As the day progresses the dust thickens. I go shopping in

Soho and buy a pink wig and some handcuffs, everything else looks tacky. Drink a little coffee, eat a little fruit, smoke a little joint.

• • •

The night is so young, not even dark yet but the dusk is threatening it so. I take the tube to Camden after work in Soho and meet Alex at the tube station after I've been standing with waifs and strays for a while in the wind as I got there too early. We embrace and trip off toward Proud Galleries happily as it feels like forever since I last saw Alex. Alex suggests we go to the Cuban bar next to Proud as he's fading away and buys me a Ché Rebellion cocktail, which is actually more expensive than his meal, but is amazing. The big painting of Ché looks down in disapproval at the sight of the price tag but don't hate the drinker, hate the bar.

Then we go to Proud. It has an Alice in Wonderland theme, lots of poseurs. We start imitating the people there and I say, "Like, *where* are all the famous people?" and Alex says, "Behind you," because a notorious boy in a band is sitting all alone on a bench next to us. So we join him. He's friendly until he asks for a cigarette and neither Alex nor I have one, at which point he gets up and leaves before we can casually bombard him with sweet nothings.

We look and listen and quickly become a little frustrated and bored by the crowds. Although everyone's drinking or high, not many are smiling and it's all too much like awkward shuffling and I'm bored already. Pete Doherty's image is drawn across the fabric of a deck chair, along with some other icons of debauched ideals, and it's slightly insulting that people are sitting lazily in the portraits of idols but maybe that's the point. As rebellion goes, that's pretty lame though. Armchair socialism has never been so literal.

Alex and I are a little disconcerted by the hallucinogenic décor and the stags' heads painted partially in red, hanging on the wall, and wonder what we've taken. There are also big double beds all reserved for people who aren't even there. I'm not sure they even exist. Maybe it's just self-promotion. Maybe it's all a lie. Maybe it's meant to be provocative. Je ne sais pas. I don't even care. But it would have been nice to lie down. Alex says he doesn't like stupid VIP beds taking up the floor space.

We're so bored that we don't bother speaking to anyone else, just gaze around. There are fake green leaves the color of cider bottles fluttering in the breeze like an artificial Eden, several TV screens showing *Alice in Wonderland* in various shades of neon and huge toadstools. There are weird support bands that nobody is watching. There is a lack of absinthe. And a red chandelier. Outside we wander, and tread onto beer-stained fake grass and hear a train rattle past the rooftops and it's all pretty. Turns into a bit of a crush, like a garden party painted by some artist on acid, and we're the spectators and props at once. There's a sign that says "Drink Me" and another, behind the bar, that says "Nothing But Liquid (On Pain of Death)" that we spend awhile trying to understand.

Alex and I wander upstairs to another more secret part of the club, which is way quieter and less crushed by poseurs. But not for especially long. We haven't been looking at the photographs hidden by pale chiffon and the rock 'n' roll portraits for long before the barman changes the music to something bad and all the crowds from below filter in "Like flies to shit" says Alex.

We're about to leave because we're sick of waiting for the band. But then Dragonette starts that minute.

They're very cute, very camp and sort of glamorous, their sound is less sharp live. But they're endearing, they're sort of touching . . . and having fun, even if the short Irish man next to me is not: "You're CRAP!" he declares, and Martina, the lead, is a little pissed off. But she recovers and the Irish man drinks some more. The air smells of stale beer and sweat and I feel sad about the smoking ban. "Where's the cloud? Where's the atmosphere?" asks Alex.

Aside from the smoking issue, all is good, except that Alex and I feel we've been transported to the eighties. It's not just that the band sounds like Duran Duran, or that everyone's a bit affected by the eighties revival in fashion. It's just the vibe. Just as I whisper to Alex, "I feel like I'm in the eighties . . .," a man walks in front of us wearing a T-shirt that says "Tour of 1984" . . . that *exact* second. And then Alex says, "Where did the last twenty years go?" And I say, "Have I been born yet?"

"Yes, darling, you were born yesterday."

ALICE

The sky is drenched in a smoggy autumnal hue at eleven a.m. when I wake from a dream about swimming in a pool and then sinking below, following Harry lower and lower, able to breathe . . . I wake up feeling tired.

I check my phone to find nothing from Harry, then reach for my Marlboro Lights and light up disheartened.

It's getting to be too much. There are other men in London after all. There are so many men I could be attracted to.

Only I'm not.

Everything I try fails . . . and it's my fault, I started it, I left the messages and cried at the wrong moment and lied at the wrong moment, and, really I should stop . . .

So I cut another line and stop those thoughts and don't care so much and think, *There are just so many men in London* . . . Feel the rush, light up a cigarette and forget about Harry.

• • •

I've been invited to a fashion show to launch a new store of some amazing American designer. I haven't really been planning to go, but see the invitation on my desk and think, why not? And call up Marina, because she's an intern at *Vogue* and appreciates couture.

"That sounds fun, Alice, I'll be there—four, did you say? Okay, shall I come to yours or meet you there? Can't wait, lots of love!"

I open a new bottle of vodka and take a swig, my mouth burning . . . I put on the Rapture and dance around in my panties and Jimmy Choos, gold stilettos, laughing to myself and feeling defiant and happy and careless and reckless and thinking about fashion and getting excited about London Fashion Week, which now seems like something big and exciting and I feel special even though before the thought bored me. I start trying on outfits—some Chanel, a little Dior sundress, my favorite aviators, my favorite beads . . . Cut another line, turn the music up, call Marina, "Oh my God, Marina, I am so excited, so excited that we should so totally have a little soirée to celebrate the new collections, come over! And bring people, we should so totally have a party!"

"Sure, I'll come now—but maybe have the party after? Like we can have the after-party? That would be so fun. I'll call people, cool, love you!"

I get bored of the Rapture so switch to Nirvana and start trying on cocktail dresses and mussing up my hair wondering if grunge will have a revival anytime soon. Then I find a French dance pop club record that I like only because I think French people sound sexy, though I'm feeling confused, and try on Chanel again feeling the vibe, *I'm so getting the collective consciousness . . . French, French clothes . . . and a yearning for the past . . . This works . . . This so totally works . . . Need another line . . . One more . . . Line . . . Mine . . .*

• • •

It's two p.m. and I'm in my bikini, have turned the heating up and am listening to a mix of a song I liked when I was fourteen or so—"Pure Shores" by All Saints—that was in *The Beach* when I had a crush on Leo DiCaprio . . . *I should go to Thailand, with Marina, that would be so fun, we'd find the island and dance . . .*

I hear the doorbell, so I run downstairs, and let Marina in . . .

"Alice, what are you doing? Is this a beach party?"

"Yea, closest to, come in! I thought, I'm just going to bring Ibiza to my bedroom."

"Can I have some?"

"Oh yeah, sure, come up, come up."

And Marina follows me up to my bedroom—covered in fashion posters and cards and pictures and photographs, and some modern Japanese décor on account of my love of the film *Lost in Translation* awhile ago . . . I put on Primal Scream's "Some Velvet Morning," cut up another gram and Marina sniffs a couple lines and we start dancing together and then Marina tries on clothes and it isn't very long before we're meant to leave for the show, and I say to Marina, who needs me, "Just wear Chanel, you can never go wrong with Chanel, black and white, and some cute shoes. Every time. Works."

And it does. We kill it, make our entrance and quickly take advantage of the attention and champagne and smile for the camera, and I say to Marina, "Is it just me? Or are the flashes of camera like really orgasmic?"

"Just you, Alice, and every model, actress, and socialite . . . Trip to the powder room, non?"

● ● ●

So much champagne and gold and high, high heels and lips painted like Russian Dolls, where ideal becomes flesh, where a painting by Rousseau inspires a cocktail dress and ethical fashion can save the world. Lingerie is more important than architecture, and hats are tools of diplomacy and war alike. I walk around and around amidst casual lights and vanity and blasé glamour for another day at work . . . The performance then brightened by the flash, flash, flash!—of cameras shooting not only the artistic marvels draped over waifs and nymphs, but also shooting down the apparent demons of the fashion world—beauty that hurts, killer heels that quite possibly could kill, and expressions so deadly that the paparazzi have to check their lenses for cracks. Estrogen, cocaine and hard sells—overkill—but it doesn't matter, because the whole thing, bad as it is, is also a sort of dream, the kind so extraordinary that to wake would only be a disappointment. I never want to come down from this height.

It is too rich and it is too thin. And yet you keep buying the pictures, the clothes, keep selling your soul, because it looks so good.

The Devil may wear Prada—but the devil, they say, is within God's grand design.

I pick out a Marlboro Red upon this thought, but find that my leopard-print lighter is tragically no longer working.

Magically it seems, a man appears with one, right beside me. He is very good-looking, and holds a little red lighter that says INFERNO on it.

"I'm Marco," he says. He has a perfect face, unnaturally white teeth, is dressed well, has a tempting smile.

"I'm Alice—and I love your suit, is that Prada you're wearing?"

There are so many men in Italy . . .

"Yes, it is, good eye . . ."

"Thank you—you have beautiful eyes, too."

"Oh, thank you—are you okay?"

"Yeah, fine, just . . ."

Marco catches me as I pass out . . . I wake up and I'm outside . . . I see the world shift and darkness envelop once more, and pass out again . . . Then come around again . . . "You need a doctor."

"No, I don't, just another line."

Marco sighs and I feel slightly guilty.

"Come on, wake up. Wake up, Alice."

"No."

"Here's some water."

"Thanks."

I sip some water, feel the world shift, then vomit into a rosebush. Marina turns up. "Alice, are you sick?"

"Just a little."

"Oh."

"I should leave. Marina, can you hail me a cab?"

"Yeah, yeah."

She comes back ten minutes later. "Ok, he's on the street, come on."

I try to walk in a way that looks balanced, and achieve it pretty well, until I fall into the cab. Marina gives the cab the address and then shuts the door.

"Marina? Marina, what are you doing? Stay with me! Don't leave—me . . ."

"Sweetie, I have to stay, career obligations, yeah?— Love you!"

●   ●   ●

The cab drops me at my door and I crawl upstairs feeling delicate and miserable. Nobody is home as usual and I'm relieved. Feeling a sudden wave of nausea, I collapse over the loo seat and cry as I throw up.

After a while I get back up and light a cigarette, take off my Chanel and pearls and pretty lingerie and cry, drink a glass of water, brush my teeth and climb into bed and try to think . . . but only fall a long way through my sheets into an exhausted, enveloping dream.

HARRY

High in a basement flat in Hackney having flashbacks to a summer I spent in California when I was sixteen. And in my flashbacks I'm having flashbacks.

I lie out in the sun and with some friends fall in love with light and air. We sit in a secluded area of the beach under a shady tree, get a little higher, and sit around for a while looking at the constellations of light like shards of glass between the leaves in the sky and the wisps of cloud that whisper in the wind before parting after the sun has moved way across the sky and it is late afternoon.

    I go back to my room and lie on the bed and all the walls move away and float. To the left the dull gray wall with light spilling in shafts through the blinds gives way and there is a blue sky with white clouds and the walls float away. The music is soft and I can hear all the instruments. I like the way the shapes in the world are. I can hear water in the music splash. There is a boat somewhere and a light bigger than the sun. The light doesn't make anyone's eyes sore. The grass is pale like that Monet painting and all the shapes are clean. I remember the summer in Biarritz, the hot gray ground with shadows, the blue sea and crowded beach. My mother drinks under an umbrella, white wine maybe. I want to be by the blue pool and to lie in the sun. It is all blue, yellow and terra-cotta, and maybe gray and navy, but so pale that the colors, the objects aren't even dark. I like being happy and being where the Beatles are forever.

I remember Montreal—it was clean. People should just be happy, the criminals, too. People should smile if they are victims and feel pleasure like when we went swimming in November when we were younger and pretended the water was hot, but it was cold and our feet went blue.

When I'm in Hackney, I'm never really in Hackney. That's why I love Hackney. And probably why Hackney puts up with me.

———————

A couple hours later I'm feeling sort of sober again, and Leo comes over and wants to talk about politics, and I say, "I don't even want to think," and light up a Marlboro instead. Leo says, "You're pathetic," and leaves, and I light up another joint as sultry dusk descends and deepens the shadows.

I'm thinking the usual stream of senseless drivel . . . that religion is like a clock but it isn't necessary to know the time. The sky is bigger than that. I can see a little clock in a big pale blue sky. A clock is subjective to time. The clock is only one way. There could be other measures of time, like time could be measured in musical notes and you could say, I'll be five quavers, and people could change the length of a beat and all the people would have to move into it. They already do that, the movie editors. It's like playing with the pendulum in a big clock.

I feel so happy and the powder-blue sky crashes through all the walls and I float in it and feel an aching feeling that I ignore because of all the white sunshine.

ALICE

Come closer . . .
        It's Harry's father again . . .
He beckons me through the mirror and I walk through it and
find myself in a room. I can't remember who anyone is, though
I have a feeling I've seen them before. I hear Charlie again,
"Come closer" . . . And I walk toward him, to the balcony.

We both stand on the balcony, smoking. I notice that
Charlie still looks a little too London Face, but I don't say
anything because I don't think he'd like it. I look down into
the moving traffic below and all the beautiful arrangements
of lines and the idea of suicide gets old because I like staring into the night sky enough not to throw myself into it. I
smoke a black clove and watch how it smolders and burns
and tastes like sugar on my lips.

I talk words of nothing to a few brief encounters who
bore me immensely. I ask Charlie, as he stands looking at
the buildings smoking a cigarette, "Can't you just give me a

drug that will make me happy?" And he says, *"I'm always here for you, you know that, Alice . . ."*

The air is all soft, playful and affectionate. The angst and intimidation have blown away and now a cool nonchalance with a caressing perfume presents itself in the air and people smile and dance along with the allure of the masquerade.

I love the baritones and blues and gold in the dust. The twilight is heady and the night indigo and calm. I take a cab with Charlie. I'm dressed as a Charlie's Angel, because we're going to a costume party, and I'm Charlie's favorite angel.

It is dark now and cold outside, when we stand outside meeting people and talking. I take a drag of a cigar from a priest. I talk to a cop, say hi to a doctor. There are a lot of French maids. We get inside eventually and start dancing. I dance with a pirate, dance with a ranger. Everyone looks good: there are prisoners, robbers, firemen, doctors and nurses, Tom Cruise, soldiers, Goldilocks, Little Red Riding Hood, the Big Bad Wolf, a white rabbit, cats, priests, nuns, the Queen of Hearts, Peter Pan and Tinkerbell, a ballerina looking faint . . . A girl helps me straighten my wig and I give her a cigarette and a smile in return. I go to sit out with some boys called Patrick and Peter. I meet a mafia gangster and stay with him for a while. Our outfits go together and so do we. We stay together until suddenly there is nobody left and we are stranded in the parking lot, as everyone else just drives away. It is getting cold and the gangster lets me wear his pinstripe gangster jacket and I give him a beer from my purse, and I call Tom Cruise who picks us up after a bit. The Big Bad Wolf has been angry for some reason and doesn't give us a ride. The air is soft and indigo. Tom Cruise picks up a French maid and Goldilocks who are caught up elsewhere.

The bourbon nocturne fades soft and high. I fall asleep and wake up a second later in a soft bed with a pink duvet and lace pillows and I look out the window but it is still dark outside. I gaze out at another touching sky, light subtle in the dim sparks of stars. A boy lying next to me hands me a cigarette and says, "It makes you high for thirty seconds, higher than you've ever been in your life, and then, nothing, and you wonder if it was even worth it. But it was."

And I reply, "Don't you just love cigarettes?"

Charlie is back again, he's standing on the balcony outside my window.

"You've got voice-mail, Alice."

He hands me my phone and I listen to the message:

"Hey, this is Kiki, and I just wanted to let you know, that like, people here have histories, and I know you're not from here, but like, people have feelings for each other, from like, three, four years of high school. For example, Mary and Peter—Jamie and Katy—Rachel and Tom—and I heard that you got on Peter, and Jamie, and Tom, and I just wanted to let you know that, I know you're clueless and everything, and you know nothing, but people have feelings here. So, if you want to talk to me about it, you can call me back. Okay, bye."

"Who are these people, Charlie?"

"People who don't like you very much."

"What should I do?"

"I don't know, take a line, go for a swim."

"Yeah, I'm going to swim in a straight line."

And then I climb onto the balcony and climb over and balance. I look at the length of the pool from above—the pale green sensual lake, suburban perimeters but reflecting from its surface moonlight. I think it looks so still and perfect, doubt diving for a moment, moved by the quiescence. But pools are meant to be disturbed, and I point my right foot and spring into the air with a breath, step into the pool, and surge into the ice water, which immediately warms and caresses, makes me happy with a shock, covers me in a light sense of gravity and ease. I emerge and breathe, take another breath and submerge again, swimming in harmony with the water and soft supple gravity, surrounded by pale blue and brushed shadows, luminous tones of gray. The water caresses and I feel no dirt on my skin, the sky burns scarlet.

A nocturne is playing the evening to sleep. There are very few stars and a discreet moon high above. I notice that the lights are off outside, but the light is on inside the water, making it luminous and pale. There is no breeze in the air, only the residue of a hot day in the damp humidity. I drop into the depths again before swimming and emerging in the center of the pool. It is subtle as the moon and still, and I dive into the depths of the placid shadow. The cicadas fade elsewhere and I hear only water splashing and my own breath. The night is still, and I like being only physical.

I dive below again and fall into the mellow shadows and float, and as I am free-falling into the depths I notice that Harry is there and I try to speak, but I can't because I'm underwater. I swim toward him but suddenly am aware of someone pulling me away from him and notice that it is Charlie, and scream but there is no sound, and Harry drifts away. Charlie puts me into a cage on the ocean's bed and locks it and goes to find Harry. And although I can see him, he can't see me, because his mask has turned into a blindfold, and I hear Charlie say, "*Come closer*", and he leads

Harry away . . . And I look around and begin to cry, and then realize there is a clock attached to the railings, and it is ticking fast, faster than it should, faster and faster and faster, and I wonder if it is a bomb as it goes: *Tick, tick, tick, tick, tick, tick, tick, tick, tick, tick, tick* . . .

And I wake, and it is nine a.m., London time.

Thursday, July 12

HARRY

I thought you were dead . . ."
   I'm falling into the smoky gray eyes of my father, his figure possessing the room, my eyes, my soul weakened with the sadness.

The badness.

"I never really died, Harry."

"I went to your funeral—you died of a heart attack—we scattered your ashes into a kilo of cocaine, like you requested in your will. You said we wouldn't get the inheritance otherwise. So your remnants were channeled into nervous systems across the capital."

"Exactly. I never really died." He's leaning against the wardrobe with an easy decadent demeanor. He's not all there but he's convincing me otherwise, like he always did. He's wearing a suit and a white shirt, and my eyes hurt as I try to look through his vaguely opaque figure . . . His eyes distract me like flames in the dark misty room.

"What does *really died* mean then? I saw you lying without a pulse."

"*What does reality mean to you, Harry?*"

"What are you trying to do to me?"

"*I'm trying to talk to you.*"

"You're too late, then—why didn't you try to talk to me when you were still alive?"

"*Listen to me—I never really died. My spirit lives on. I'm all around you.*"

"Why are you here then?"

"*I want you to help me.*"

"How?"

"*I asked you what reality meant to you. I'm here to tell you. Reality, Harry, is what killed me.*"

"But you said you never really died."

"*In reality, I am dead—in other ways, I am very much alive.*"

"I don't understand."

"*Yes, you do. You're my son—and I've been watching you—and know you know as well as I do that reality is a flexible thing. We can defy it. We can change it—we can reverse what has happened and determine the future.*"

"How can we defy it?"

"*Just listen to me.*"

"I'm listening."

"*Reality poisoned me, Harry, it was my enemy all my life, and in the end, it shifted me into the outer realms.*"

"I can't believe I'm hearing this."

"*You'd better believe it. It's who you are.*"

I don't answer.

"*You're an escapist, you're a rebel.*"

"This is ridiculous. I'm hallucinating."

"Maybe. But that doesn't make me any less real, does it?"

I don't answer for a while.

"What does it mean then? What are you trying to say?"

"I'm telling you that there are many possible realities, dimensions, whatever you want to call it—there are so many different ways, Harry. Some ways are better than others. You know that. You know that figments of your imagination make more sense than a sober traipse down through this godforsaken city . . . We've been lumbered with a cruel world, a cruel reality . . . But the war's not over yet: we can defy reality. It killed me in so many ways, and I want revenge."

"Revenge on reality?"

"Yes."

"How?"

"There are infinite ways to destroy reality, Harry. Take your pick."

"What's the point?"

"To avenge my cruel death."

"But you said you never really died."

"I never completely died, but part of me did. My soul lives on. I exist in some spheres. But it's not enough. I want more, Harry. I want to defy death, defy reality. And only you can really help me."

"By destroying reality?"

"It's what you're best at."

"A revolution?"

"Exactly."

"A revolution against reality?"

"You've been fighting it for years without realizing it. You know what you have to do."

"Actually, I'm not so sure I do."

"Do you know the dangers of dalliance?"

And with that, Charlie is gone, nothing to prove his momentary visit but a fading cloud of dirty smoke.

Where am I? I look around . . . Just a basement somewhere in North London with glass shattered on the ground and smoke fading like a genie set loose from his bottle.

ROSE

I'm thinking about Alice as I walk home, wondering why she's turned into such a mess, how I'm not so different really.

I'm remembering how different she was only a year earlier, close to when she broke up with Hugo and just before she ran off with Harry. There had been a brief time when she had seemed free and footloose and fun, the girl I grew up with, before all the illusions, delusions, confusions, before Alice started running away in every possible and impossible direction.

We went out together, in August, when things were starting to look up, when the autumn was freshening the sky, before she went back to Manhattan, and there was a feeling of charm and imminent adventure.

After tapas in Soho, we went to Koko in Camden Town around eleven. The first time we lined up we were turned away because Alice forgot her ID. So we went back to Kensington then returned to Koko, when the queue had tripled. We didn't want to queue, so stood by the entrance and the doorman beckoned us forward and swiftly let us in. Alice showed him her passport, the photo taken when she was sixteen. "It's a young photo," she explained, "three years ago."

"Yes," he replied, "a much younger photo."

"A lot happened in a few years," and he smiled and let us in.

Inside, a band was playing and there were crowds of people on the dance floor below and also crushed onto all the balconies and at the several bars tucked into corners of the club. Everywhere seemed red, and everyone was very well dressed, in a glamorous grungy way, all disheveled so carefully, fragmented piece by expensive piece, a crowd of kids doing the heroin chic thing that had been going on since the nineties, kids who would never touch the stuff in real life. Some of them were bona fide addicts, perhaps, but most of them looked too healthy for that.

Alice and I drank vodka with lemonade and walked around noticing people and making an impression where appropriate. Alice was wearing a blue dress, vintage and from a French shop in Camden, bare legs and black heels, with a cigar-box handbag. I was wearing a black dress with velvet gray and silver heels and pretty jewelry. We had not made that much effort, but it seemed to work.

We went into a room with little booths and tables and different music playing, something vaguely electronic, and smoked cigarettes, then sat down with two boys. Alice talked to one boy who turned out to be very irritating, and I talked briefly to another boy who turned out to be a very good

*kisser, and I got a little carried away, but when in Koko,
that's okay . . . Alice talked to some boys in the band . . .
We lost each other, found each other again around two a.m.,
picked up our coats from the cloakroom and disappeared
into the night . . . Took random buses because we wanted
to explore some more, then got a little disoriented around
Kentish Town, traveled south to the soundtrack of junkies
tripping out and telling ridiculous stories, little boys stoned
and wide-eyed—and then got a little lost around Piccadilly
and in the end shared a cab back to Kensington.*

*"You know, this has been so much fun. I should go out
single more often!" said Alice with a glow.*

"So is it over with Hugo?" I asked hopefully.

*"I don't know . . . He's kind of addictive." She said it
mischievously . . . He was really too old for her and although he was attractive I didn't really understand it. I didn't
really understand if Alice was addicted to Hugo or something else . . .*

"That's why you should stop."

ALICE

Who's chasing you, Alice?"
    "Charlie, leave me alone. No one's chasing me."
I'm back in my bedroom and looking through stacks of
CDs looking for something to distract from the voice in my
head—*Radiohead? No—Talking Heads? No* . . . Where are
my other CDs, where are they? I can't see.

"Sad, isn't it, that no one's chasing, nobody cares."
    "Leave me alone."
    "I'm always here for you—you know that."
    "Leave me alone. I want to be alone."
    "You'll never be alone. You've got a child now."
    "No, I don't."
    "What are you going to call him?"
    "She doesn't exist."
    "Boy or girl, it's got a name already."
    "No, it doesn't."
    "I'll never leave you, Alice."

"Stop. Leave me alone."

"I can't leave you."

"Why not?"

"Because I'm part of you."

"No, you're not."

"Yes, I am. Your child's name is Charlie. I'm part of you now."

"Leave me alone."

"I can't leave you alone. I need you, and you need me."

"Stop this, Charlie, I want you to leave."

"It's too late now."

I run to the bathroom and throw up, and can't stop throwing up . . .

"You love me, Alice . . . Who's chasing you now?"

HARRY

Already taken, already used. I can't feel anything anymore. Sometimes I lie awake at night and want her, but also know I am only using her, like one more cheap thrill. It breaks me to know I value her so low. Value myself even lower.

But I don't know how else to live, think, dream . . . I'm dropping. When high I'm ecstatic, blissfully unaware of my life crumbling, but I'm moving further away, caring less every day, losing sight, losing mind, losing will. I'm caught in this loop. It exhausts me. I feel I've lived a thousand lives, been through heaven and hell a million times, and it seems not to matter. I cannot grasp anymore what it is I'm supposed to do, what I could possibly do within this blur that would matter.

Each day I've heard before.

Top up the same old glass and drink again.

In the hope that one of these days I'll just pass out, drift off, escape my great escape . . . Break the glass . . . And never drink again.

ALICE

I take a Xanax to mellow my anxiety and forget Charlie and Harry and sleep, because I'm so tired it's making me crazy, and fall into a half sleep, a dreamlike contemplation, my thoughts streamlined and my mind detached, watching from above . . .

Watching the view of Manhattan from above . . .
Watching a view of myself from above.

"I just want to say good-bye one more time," I told Harry on the plane.

"Do you say good-bye a lot?"

"I've been saying it a lot recently."

"Just to Manhattan?"

"No."

What was I leaving? . . . What was I chasing?

• • •

I went to Manhattan so that I could find something else—
not the boys at school, not myself as I had previously been—
but other characters, other people, a vague ideal of myself
better than at present, a little higher, a little older.

In New York, so I had been told so many times, everybody walks with purpose and everyone knows where they
are going and they go there fast. And if you don't know
where you're going, then you are just lost, and New York
is not a good place to get lost in, if you want to be found
again.

Sometimes I didn't think so much about logical literal
things. If you're going to get lost, I used to think, then it may
as well be in Manhattan—it seemed more fashionable somehow, than being lost anywhere else. Or London—anywhere
with kudos and height and high society and low society I
could lose myself in. It was a new life I had wanted to find
and make up, an ideal with which to ignore the reality of
the past. I didn't have to think about my mother or father or
the feeling that something was missing, because New York
shifted the focus onto other things.

I found I liked distractions, intimidating men with girl-
friends and Marlboro Reds, a hell of a lot of tension and
the air thick with tobacco. It was fun, that rare time when
I forgot all about the sad stories and instead simply smiled
and smoked, intimidated and intimidating, and nothing else
even crossed my mind.

Perhaps my main problem was that I never stopped wanting
more than seduction from Manhattan or London or anywhere
else. I wanted more—wanted love—chased and chased . . .

"But you found me instead," whispers Charlie.

————

I was meant to meet with a new acquaintance in a café in Chelsea but as I climbed the steps up from the subway on West Twenty-third Street I realized I couldn't do it anymore. I tried to pull myself together but I didn't feel the same energy I felt before.

I walked away from the café and east to Fifth then all the way to the UN Plaza, cutting through all the avenues and traffic and people, my face faded and legs sore, regretful somehow and feeling only ambiguous impulses. I kept walking and walking because I did not want to stop, still had some ingenuous residual ambition, some trace of aimless, reckless passion that was Manhattan's lifeblood it seemed.

I was lost in lifeblood. I kept running around the arteries and veins of Manhattan in a pulse, a drive, a new verve caught from the compel of deviation, and looking for something else.

I took the subway back down to Twenty-third and went into a coffee shop near Madison Square Park. I bought a coffee and sat down, and then said to the attractive man next to me, "Will you mind my coffee?" while I went to the restroom.

Upon my return, we started talking:

"Thank you," I smiled, sitting down again.

"I had to fight off hordes of men."

"I can imagine."

"Had to fight them away, fearing the wrath of a woman without her coffee."

I smiled and introduced myself, and he replied, "I'm Tom."

Tom turned out to be a CEO from Boston, in New York on business. I told him about the audition I failed that day.

"So do you want to do films or the stage?"

"Both, probably films more, but there's something about the stage."

I found it good and reassuring to talk to him, he was about forty maybe and with dark brown hair.

Then his colleague came in and told a story about how he had once walked through a Sex and the City set by mistake and screwed up the production.

"Right here, on Madison Square, there were film crews everywhere and I didn't even notice until they told me to move."

"Guess I'd better go then, it was great meeting you," I said.

"It was great meeting you, too. Good luck with the acting."

I shot a coy "Thank you" and left.

At night, I lay on a single bed with blue sheets and the gray shadows in the room were calm and soft. The gauze floated in the air from the breeze that delicately blew outside and through the open window. There was a pot plant on the table near the window and its leaves stirred gently. Black and white striped cushions were stacked on a chair and the lines crossed over one another. My suitcase was on the floor, my shoes were scattered a little, and the breeze blew billows into the chiffon some more.

Acting wasn't working, relationships weren't working . . .

• • •

I met a student from some liberal arts college in Massachusetts who was tall with dark hair and glasses and had a calm

expression and voice, and we told each other our life stories
as the train paused for a while.

"I'm in high school, in Connecticut, just here for a week.
It's so good just to get out and be alone for a while."

"With all the millions of Manhattan?"

"Oh I don't mind them . . ."

"So do you want to come to college here after high school
then?"

"Maybe . . . If I go to college. I think I'll take a year out
to decide what to do. Maybe acting, maybe fashion—who
knows?"

"Take a year off, I wish I had . . ."

"Really?"

"Yeah, because I'm at college, but I hate my courses and
I still have no direction, and I'll probably end up repeating a
year—so I may as well have taken a year off."

"So you think I should just drift for a while?"

"Drift, sure . . . But make it work in the end."

• • •

On Saturday, I went to an art exhibition opening in a loft
apartment in Chelsea and met a nice Italian man who told
me all about New York, especially Little Italy, and taught
me how to pronounce his name. We sat in chairs away
from the crowd and talked about our families, looked at
noir photographs, and ate olives. "If you're ever in LA,
come visit with me—it's where I am now. I can show you
around."

After all the flux died down I went for a walk outside. A
few doors down from the apartment there was a nightclub
called Prey where there was a huge line of people outside,
two limos and a beat-up silver car. I walked by and went to

Madison Square Park under a full moon, wishing I didn't have to ever go home from this pretty, pretty play.

Maybe I don't, I thought—and I called that man I met a couple months ago at the Beautiful and Damned party . . . Why not?

ROSE

Alice, is everything okay? You don't look good . . ." I walk in to find Alice in bed with photos scattered around and a vacant expression, her eyes unfocused and spaced out.

"I'm just remembering when I was happy . . ." she says.

"Well why aren't you happy now?"

"I'm trying to remember where it all went wrong. And I don't know. I was happy in New York and school was okay. And my first gap year was fun. I think it all started falling to pieces when I started dating Hugo."

"And you started doing drugs?"

"No, I did drugs before that," her tone faint and fatigued. "Everything just lost its novelty, though, in my second gap year. All the parties started to feel the same."

"Well that's when most people find something sustainable—like university, or a job."

"Yeah, it's when most people grow up. But I don't want to."

There is a pause. Alice continues.

"And it's at that point, when there's nothing new to try, that you try the same things for a third time, and a fourth time, and then a night out just isn't fun without a line or a pill, and then you find yourself staying with some loser not because you love him, but because you love his cocaine. And then the months flutter by and you realize you can't stop them fluttering by while you watch detached as your life becomes a joke."

She looks back at me as if suddenly remembering again that I exist.

"Who let you in?"

"The cleaner."

"I told her not to let anybody in. I'm tired. I need to be alone. I'll call you. But can you just leave now?" Alice looks away, not interested in a reply.

"Sure. Sorry, I'll phone you later, okay?"

"Sure."

Alice wants space so I decide to visit Harry, as much to check he's still alive as anything else.

ALICE

W hy not?"

I couldn't think of any persuasive reasons why not. I could only think that: *This could be my Something More . . .*

Hugo preyed on my weakness . . . Chased my weakness . . . Like I wanted him to . . .

Pray to your weakness . . . Worship your weakness . . .

"Meet me in the bathroom," he said.

Meet me in the bathroom, he said, meet me in the bathroom, meet you in the bathroom, I liked that song, it reminded me of when I saw the Strokes play a year earlier, how I danced all night and fell in love with the boys and the blur . . . *Meet me in the bathroom . . . He said, meet me in the bathroom* . . . I wait by myself for a while, then Hugo comes back and cuts me a line, and some time passes and I keep going back for more, until I'm alone again with my own little stash, and someone or something else to meet with me in the bathroom:

"Hello Alice . . . I'm Charlie."

I recognized the man who stood in front of me from the papers—he was found Not Guilty of indulging and dealing in guilty pleasures . . .

"Weren't you in the papers? Didn't you die?"

"No, I'm alive . . . We're all so alive . . ."

HARRY

I lie on a beach as the sun sets near midnight on a Newquay midsummer night, and fall into a dream, and I lie here and sprinkle handfuls of sand slowly over my body, seeing simultaneously every thought and dream fall apart into tiny fragments I cannot see after they fall. After two hours I have buried myself in fragments, and Leo helps me up and tells me that maybe smoking that is not a good idea anymore. "But there are no good ideas anymore."

Being distracted, albeit never satisfied, has a kind of harmless anarchy to it, and there is something fun about doing stupid things because they look and feel good, and not making any sense but saying it with enough allure to be entertaining. "Ban Smoking, it's harmful to other people," they say. "No, Ban Passive Smoking," they reply.

There are so many rules and so much general advice that the rules have an anarchy of their own, and the only way to deal with it is to devise a new line of thought where the rule is to jump higher and from above you can look down and figure out the urbanity and inanity and insanity, and suddenly understand the wider scheme of things. Only there is no wider scheme of things that makes any more sense than what is already apparent. Heaven and Hell are not that distant to think about when there are images of war (accepted by authority) on televisions in cafés twenty-four hours a day and junkies sing songs of paradise (prohibited by authority) on the radio at the same time.

It's all such an incomprehensible daze,
   Just empty wineglasses and ash in trays . . .

• • •

I sleep for a couple hours, waking in a sweat, and reach out for a half-empty bottle of vodka. My throat is dry and I have mouth ulcers from smoking so much. Nevertheless, I pull out another Marlboro and listlessly light up and smoke to calm my nerves. I'm so sick of the dreams, want nothing more anymore than to sleep without interruption from my tormented subconscious . . . always obsessed with pills, kills, thrills, these days. *When did all the drama get so dull? What did I dream anyway?*

I stub out my cigarette on the wooden floor and light up another, vaguely thinking that at some point in the day I will have to visit my mother because my father told me to. But I'm distracted, by Leo, by the wardrobe with the burn marks, feeling listless and yet strangely sober. The more I wake up, the more I feel it again, the aching in my head, my bones, my eyes, my skull, the aching that reminds me I'm still alive. *Why am I waiting? Why can't I just leave? Where would I go?* I think dispassionately of all the places in the world.

I could just disappear.

I could go anywhere, just pack up and leave. What's stopping me?

I begin to cry silently, still, alone, dissolute. I can't leave this little room, this little mess I have got myself into. I can't leave my dealer, my dependence on an increasingly dull euphoria.

This isn't fun anymore. This is nothing, this is hell. And it was always going to happen. When I was twelve I was waiting to leave. This was always going to happen. I wanted out from the beginning, and this was the best exit.

So why is it taking so long?

Why don't I just bow out before it gets worse? Why don't I just take my exit? What's stopping me?

I think of Alice, think of my mother, think of Leo. They'd hate me for it. I'd be a perpetual failure in their eyes. They would remember me as a failure and nothing more.

I pour some red wine into a glass.

Haven't completely lost my manners, then . . .

Thoughts of the pain I would cause pause me. But there is something worse to fear.

If Charlie is still around, though he should have died, then what's to say it wouldn't happen to me? What's to stop him tormenting and punishing me forever? If I let him down and died now, he'd make me pay. There are other spheres, is what he said. He's in all of them, so no matter whether I live or die, he will find me.

———————

Harry's mother had taken to using her maiden name again, which reminded her of when she was free and twenty-two, when she was the very pretty Kate Marlborough. She was chasing lost youth in other ways—the Botox, the yoga, the range of disgusting herbal teas, the seaweed wraps and retreats in Peru. She looked very glamorous and fresh, but in her eyes, in her occasional tears, she was sad. Life was passing her by. She felt hard done by even though she wasn't, not by anyone else's standards.

She was lonely and sad though and the drugs had lost their magic long ago. She sometimes played with the idea of returning to New York, the playground of her youth, but Harry was right when he said that Manhattan got bored of you, but London never tires of a fraud—and she knew it too. That's why she stayed in London—it propped her up against all odds. There was always someone to go to lunch with, there was always another fashion show, there was always the attention of her old friends. There was always the moonlight crying rain over the gloaming dark Thames. She loved the place, probably more than anything else. It was the only relationship that lasted.

She could look out into the city and feel it mirror herself. It was beat and it was blue, but nevertheless it bore a kind of beauty, a Blitz spirit lighting up the damp miserable scene.

As Harry approached the flat, uncomfortable with the dirty white façades of Knightsbridge, incongruous to the grandeur of the backdrop buildings, he saw his mother in the window, pale and thin and delicate. She looked like she wanted to be somewhere else, looked like in her mind she was already somewhere else. In a way therefore she looked like Charlie.

She heard Harry unlock the door, but stayed standing by the window.

———

"Mum . . ."

She turns to face me. I can't smile. She's pale and rough beneath the makeup, and barely concealing despair.

"How *are* you?" she says brightly.

"Don't."

"Don't? Sorry?" She can hardly speak.

"Don't say what you always, always say. Don't act like you care when it's obvious you don't."

"Harry, don't be ridiculous, of course I care. Don't be so rude."

"Why not?" I reply.

"Why are you so angry with me?"

"I'm sick of this. I'm sick of this stupid place, these lies, this emptiness. I'm angry because you never talk to me."

"I do, I . . ."

"Just listen to me. I'm sick of you. I've been trying to understand why I can't deal with anything anymore—and then it just came to me—it's you. You never talked to me, you never listened. You weren't here when Dad died. You didn't love him either."

"That's not fair, Harry. Of course I loved him, and I love you. What's wrong with you? This is so irrational, this is so unlike you."

"How do you know it's unlike me? You don't know who I am at all."

"Harry, you're scaring me."

"You're always scared of something. That's why you're always drunk or sedated. You can't cope. You chose pills over me a long time ago. You never loved me."

"That's ridiculous. Harry, what brought this on? What have you taken? Are you drunk?"

"No, I've just been thinking. Dad was right. You're a fraud, you're an idiot, and you're deceptive. The rumors

were true, you never loved him either. You strung us along
. . . You're so passive."

"How can you say these things to me?"

"Because they're true. And I've been playing along for
too long and I can't do it anymore. I'm sick to death of it all.
You're killing me."

"Don't be ridiculous. You're being melodramatic and
childish and I won't put up with it."

"You're the one who's ridiculous. You're trying to make
a stand but even your voice is too weak. I don't know why
I came here. There's no point. I don't want to see you again.
I hate you."

"Harry?"

I feel light-headed and tired and guilty as my mother begins to cry. I turn and leave, and run down flights of stairs
and run down the streets and don't stop running until I can't
breathe anymore, and I collapse against a wall, in the delirium
of my own despair, my mother's despair, Alice's despair, all
my fault, all my mistakes.

ALICE

It was a Monday evening in November when I arrived in Manhattan for the first time by myself, when I was sixteen, and the sea mirrored the golden sun and all the lights flared up brilliantly.

I sat in the park and smoked a cigarette and then sat in a coffee shop and saw the people out of the window. Smoke poured onto the roads and faded into the dusky sky, faded against the tall buildings and lines of mirrored windows. I met a photographer called Hilary, aged twenty, when she sat down at my table and we talked for a while. She was from northern California and had been on the road with a gypsy punk band all over the states, had just arrived in New York and decided to stay there, move indefinitely in the early spring. Her eyes were intensely pale blue and she wore a white dress over jeans, had high cheekbones and dark blonde hair tied back. She had her first commission with a magazine and was arranging the layout on her iBook. The couple sitting behind us were involved in a heated argument about acting and racism and we were intrigued until we found out it was a script they were reading through and the argument was mere fiction. "Well it is New York," she said.

Hilary told me about the band she photographed, Gogol Bordello, and the lead singer, "I ate what they ate, drank what they drank, smoked what they smoked . . ." Hilary showed me photos and we talked about how we loved New York City more than men.

Outside of the window, I looked at the slanted ceiling of the subway entrance and the shadows of railings and stairs. Two women talked and a man bent over to pick up a letter, traffic paused, people walked. Cigarette smoke mixed with the white clouds, light fumes and cosmopolitan breath, just toxic enough to give the city delirious air like no other. Then the guitarist from Gogol Bordello came in and Hilary introduced us and soon after I left the coffee shop.

Outside I walked into Union Square and there were people beating drums and walking big dogs. I went back to my room and made some coffee, called a family friend, Miguel, and arranged to go out to dinner. We ate sushi and walked through SoHo, past tattoo parlors and coffee shops and a casual movement of revelry.

• • •

Later in the week I took a cab to Bloomingdale's. Before entering I went into a small Italian coffee shop on Lexington, where the barista greeted me, "Bella, bella, every time I see you my heart—" and he mimed a beat beat. "Thanks. But you haven't seen me before." He looked confused for a few seconds. I said, "There must be lots of girls that look like me." "Oh no, I must be confusing you with another beautiful woman." He gave me a bagel with a confused smile.

The men in New York were so welcoming.

After some shopping, I hailed a cab and rode to Park Avenue to meet my godmother. I turned my phone on, to find I had lots of messages, one from my godmother's personal assistant, asking if I wanted to go to a cocktail party that evening at the British Consulate for the Royal Academy. Luckily, I happened to be wearing a pretty enough black and white dress and had scarlet Chanel lipstick in my purse.

The apartment of the British Consulate was high in the sky and had a beautiful view of the city, which was dark and sparkling. Inside the walls were white in the main room and red in the dining room. There were many works by Nigerian artists, which was where the consul had been recently. My godmother introduced me to people connected to the Royal Academy. The older ladies were the most interesting because they had high hair and haute couture.

When they left I kissed my godmother good-bye and she said, "Well you were a hit—they all loved you."

The feeling was mutual. I was high as the starry diamonds in the sky and my eyes glittered accordingly.

I took the subway to Canal with the intention of going to an Eastern European place Hilary told me about in SoHo. On the subway, there was a deranged old black man who shook coins in a Starbucks cup but whom everybody ignored. When I stepped off the train and walked along the platform two huge rats scurried past close to my stilettos. They were very big rats. They were very high heels. There was thunder, lightning and a half moon that night in the sky.

I walked the wrong way out of the subway by mistake, got lost for an hour or so in Chinatown. Eventually I asked a bouncer for directions and he told me to go all the way back about half an hour. So I did, stopping by the end for a cappuccino in Little Italy. The coffee shop was Bella Ferrera, next to Cha Cha's and Luna Restaurant, and a red Moped was parked in the street.

A fever was playing in the Bulgarian Bar, where many Eastern European immigrants were strung out in bohemian revelry. Hilary was not there, but it didn't matter because there was so much going on, music and dancing and laughter, and I felt so at ease and happy with the gypsies, immigrants and curious people that being technically alone was not significant at all. Gypsies, clowns, stripes, lipstick and laughter—and I felt such a child, so ingenuous, and yet so at home, as if I was finally in the circus troupe I had so longed to run away with. The bottles gleamed colorfully in rows behind the counter and there was a screen with Bulgarian television on it. The place was crowded and I liked the clothes and glinting jewelry girls were wearing. I sat down and watched for a bit and then danced with some random man but when he kept pushing a dubious-looking glass of red wine in my face, like some poisoned cup, I got bored and left, teasing him with a smile as I danced away and down the stairs into the street. I went down into the subway and the train moved away just as I stepped on.

•   •   •

I took trains all over Manhattan when I was there, in breaks from school in Connecticut, running around underground wherever I wanted to go, and generally finding myself somewhere else instead. I had a similar relationship with drugs—I always had an idea of where I wanted to go, but somewhere along the line got lost and ended up somewhere different—sometimes different in a good way—other times just Different.

"You seem real mellow, Alice. Have you taken some thing?"

Rosé just walked into my bedroom to see me sitting in bed watching the little reflections of light spin around the room from a disco ball I have put up. The window is open and chiffon blows around and I just stare at the patterns of light vacuously, and reply to Rosé without looking at her, in a faint and bored tone, getting sick of her overbearing voice, sounding so loud:

"I needed a Xanax. I could do with another if you don't stop nagging."

Rosé puts a hand on her hip: "It's not good for you, Alice. Be responsible, for once in your life. Just be careful."

I look Rosé straight in the eye and speak louder: "Don't tell me what to do. Don't think you can just walk in here and insult me and criticize me when I've never felt more alone or depressed in my life. You have no idea what I'm going through. You haven't got a fucking clue. You've got a place at Cambridge and supportive parents—I haven't. I've got a father who doesn't care about anything more than appearances, my mother who doesn't want to know me . . . So if I want—if I need—a pill, or a line, or a fucking cigarette, then I'll have one. And you can't stop me. You have no right to. I don't even want to see you anymore. You're a fucking lightweight and I'm sick of it. I'm sick of everything. If I want a line I'll fucking have one."

Rosé seems a little taken aback, but maybe she's getting used to it now and replies:

"Problems, Alice? You think you have problems? Darling, you don't know what depression is."

Always so fucking patronizing. I sip some more vodka

tonic and feel sad and say, "Harry doesn't want me, nobody wants me."

"I want you. But not like this."

"Well I don't want to live any other way. I can't live any other way."

"You're prepared to risk your life for cocaine? That's disgusting, Alice."

"No, you're disgusting, treating me like this. You're meant to be a friend. But you're just like everyone else—you judge me, you criticize me, you think I'm dirt."

"I'm only here and saying these things because this isn't you. You've turned into something you're not. You've changed. You used to be different. But now, you're just ungrateful and destructive and lost. And I want to help you, I really do, but you're not making it easy."

"I don't want your help. I want you to leave. Now."

"I don't want to leave you."

"You already have. You left me when you started trying to change me. You can't change me. I am what I am. You can't cherry-pick the character traits you want in me. You can't decide who I should be or might have been or could be. Because I am none of those things. I'm what you see, and you can't change it."

"You need to grow up."

"I have grown up. And I don't like what I see. And right now, I'm looking at you in particular, and you disgust me. So get the fuck out of my house and leave me alone, and forget our little trips out and all the fashion shows I took you to, because it's mine, and not yours, and soon you're going to realize that you miss it. You'll miss me. And you'll realize your life is boring and uneventful without me. But it will be too late, because I've left you, and I never want to see you again."

Rosé turns and leaves. As the door shuts, I take the little bag of cocaine from my purse and cut a couple lines and open a new bottle of vodka and take a long burning swig and light a cigarette and smash a vase of flowers at the wall and sit down against a wall and let the anger subside as I drink more, smoke more, sniff more, feel less . . .

And feel a whole lot better. *Less is more* . . .

I mix a vodka martini and put a Bowie record on and fall into another dream, a memory triggered by the euphoria of the moment, reminding me of what I have always lived for—the euphoria of the moment—what Harry has always lived for, what I would always live for, even die for, because living and dying seem to belong in the same blur anyway . . . *Living is dying is living is dying is living is dying is living* . . .

The Laughing Gas Chamber

ALICE

One Saturday just less than a year earlier, I caught the bus to Oxford. Tim, a childhood friend whom I'd known since age thirteen, met me off the bus and we walked to Banbury Road, where he had just moved into a new flat with friends, hence the party. Only a few people had arrived, and I met them and then Tim showed me to his new room, and we drank red wine and talked a little and I met some others . . .

I met a thespian called Isaac, who wore a Star of David round his neck and we talked about the theater. Then I met Mark, Tim's friend, and we talked about New York and books, and I spilled a glass of red wine all over my black dress, though it soaked in and didn't show, and all over the floor. I just pretended it hadn't happened and kept talking, and magically kitchen towels appeared on the floor and the wine was mopped up discreetly and efficiently, and I walked with Mark outside, where it was quite cold but soft and relaxed.

After going back inside, I met an Etonian called Tobias, who looked like an Adonis, with a red scarf and blond hair. As Tobias had laughing gas back in his room, I traipsed off with him, Jonny and Katy, and two boys from Malta. The boys ended up hailing a cab so they wouldn't have to walk, though it was not very far. I talked to Tobias about the film *Bright Young Things*, and the book by Evelyn Waugh.

"*Vile Bodies* is my favorite book," he said. When we got to Tobias's, I sat on the bed next to Katy and Jonny was on my right. Tobias described the laughing gas for us:

"It makes your whole body tingle," he said enthusiastically, waving his fingers. After three balloons we were all in a little euphoria, after another four I passed out. I awoke to Tobias saying, "I love it that she's so uncorrupted, so easily amused," which made me smile . . . Then Tim came in as they were lighting the bong, said, "Come on, you have two choices: you can go home with me now, and still go to acting tomorrow—or you can stay here, and—I know what Tobias is like, Alice."

(And that's why I wanted to stay . . . And yet . . .)

With a huge stretch of willpower, I struggled up, smiling. We all said we'd meet up in London . . . I walked with Tim for twenty minutes back to Banbury Road and we talked, and then Tim slept on the floor so that I could have his bed, and very kindly set his alarm for me.

I got up at 6:30 a.m. and got the 7:20 a.m. bus back to London. I was feeling quite bright considering the lack of sleep . . . I went back to Kensington and accidentally set off the house alarm, then went to acting class. It was "Acting for Camera," and seeing my face on-screen was not joyous in this hungover state, as increasingly became the case. By lunchtime, I felt close to dead, and my arm was still stained with red wine from when I spilled it all over my dress, which I hadn't had time to change.

I went straight from acting class to meet Harry in Green Park though, and as I waited for him by the tube station I tried to light a cigarette but my hands were shaking so it was a challenge. We walked through the park upon meeting, and his presence made my hangover disappear, and I noticed the bright sky and the way it lit up his eyes, and it occurred to me that I rarely saw him in the daylight. It suited him. He looked younger, disheveled, handsome.

When it got windy we went and bought coffee and talked about Velvet Underground and opium dens in Thailand. Then we walked back through the park, and sat down on the grass again and kissed some more and everything else became a mere blur in the background and I didn't want to be anywhere else ever again, didn't want it to stop.

● ● ●

Why is it that the things I want to stop won't stop and the things I want to last forever are cut short? I begin to cry as the vodka pulls me down and down, and the only way not to fall is to sniff the rest of the cocaine and call my dealer and wait for her to arrive.

ROSE

I feel hurt by Alice and tired by London so I just go home and start packing my bags. I've got a festival to be at tomorrow and the timing has never been more perfect. My friend Araminta is coming back from a choir trip tonight and then we're getting out of London tomorrow morning.

I pack the things I need: dresses, boots, sleeping bag, bikini, flip-flops, more dresses, cigarettes, phone, money, love, music, friendship, and get excited.

It's only noon though and I'm not leaving town until Saturday morning. So I take a train up to the Heath and think maybe I'll just lie around there for a bit. I bring a cute little bottle of wine and sip it through a straw and start daydreaming about the festival and the other festivals I've been to and music and magic. And Alice, and I remember a night in Soho three years ago, another summertime in London, remembering the perfume of falafel and gin and chili peppers.

• • •

A Friday night, we went to a little café bar in Soho and the place played a seductive nocturne for hours stretching slow . . . Alice's hair was long and curled, she felt like a change from straight apparently, smiling mischievously and secretively. The bar was in a small space, there was a quiet sense of communal excitement. People sat outside at round tables and the street was alight with color and people. Inside a man and a woman played guitar and sang discreetly at the far wall, and in the center of the room was a table with antipasti and almond bread laid out on a white tablecloth, with a vase of sunflowers in the middle. The walls were painted a dusky purple and the lights were warm yellow, and pictures, postcards and paintings decorated the background. In the left corner, shadows accumulated because the lighting was eclectic and inconsistent. There were also bookcases with random old books of philosophy and literature, and a large rectangular mirror where light reflected in spheres over the ceiling. All of the tables were different shapes and the chairs were crowded around, and people ate almond bread and drank coffee in small groups that were all attached to each other.

Alice ordered a vodka cranberry and I ordered a vodka lemonade. We sat down at a round wooden table by the door, because every other seat was taken. A woman gave us some almond bread and we talked about festivals in the summer, which ones to try for next year . . .

I was facing the window and could see all the lights and people reflected on the glass, a car moving by. The music was soft and did not demand attention, simply played in the background. The air smelled of coffee, cigarettes, falafel and antipasti like olives and peppers and chili somewhere. The refrigerator was covered in postcards and photographs, and cards advertising musical events were in little stacks on the counter, where a Russian man sat on a stool and tried to choose one food out of many possibilities. Cups, mugs, bowls and plates were stacked in towers up against the wall, and it all looked relaxed and calmly ordered. We were happy.

There was a poster that said: "You Want Dreads? I Can Make Them Happen." We talked about tattoos and hair colors; Alice said she wanted to get married spontaneously in Vegas someday. Fleetingly I wished I could fall in love and be married before twenty-two.

We sipped our drinks and looked around, there was a small tree planted in a large pot in the corner, where a black man with high cheekbones and dreads was with a black woman in a violet top, talking with a white woman with long dark hair, the one who offered almond bread. They all looked content and smiling. The light looked good against the purple and the cluttered décor all around.

We left an hour and a half after entering, when the people in the café were still all the same and the darkness outside had brought a subtle quietude to the euphoria. We were happy and the night was warm, as we crossed the road and walked to the underground to go to Camden. We went to see Harry's band playing in a bar, met Leo and some others, heard a little heartache, heard a little blues.

We liked the songs. We liked the cigarettes, too. Beer bottles crowded the tables pulled in a line by the edge of the audience, where friends sat and smoked. They played some new songs from the past week or so, and there was a little talking outside of the rhythm.

We were talking in between the songs and decided it would be fun to travel the Continent together, to take trains all around and get jobs in vineyards. Then we talked about taking a road trip in America and we both wanted to go to Seattle and San Francisco and Chicago and New Orleans.

"Or maybe we could take a train," said Alice, smiling with mercurial eyes, a delirious soul. We missed that train. Started taking planes instead.

HARRY

Harry's great-grandfather, on his mother's side, Jamie, was a duke's son and an officer in the Second World War after Harrow and Oxford. He smoked sixty cigarettes a day and led thirty men through battles in Cassino, Italy, with success, but for one shot lung and many shot friends.

Jamie kept smoking cigarettes though, for years after, and smoking a pipe, and smoking cigars, always with sad listless eyes, because when he came back from war, his young wife had died. They had only been married five years, and four were taken by the war. She had been killed in the Blitz.

So he'd sit around and smoke in a slumber and wait out the days, mourning the lost days, lost years, lost lives, and new wives came and went, but really his love died in the war, in Cassino, where lives were gambled away as the stakes got higher—too high, some thought—but after a point, does it matter? All you have to do is win. And life, after a while, is obsolete, when everything you cared about has gone to dust already.

Jamie's son married a rich blonde debutante from New England and had a few children who partied out the eighties, one of whom was Catherine, always called Kate—Harry's mother. She sniffed cocaine like it was roses and in so doing met, one electrical night when she was twenty-two, a man called Charlie, who spoke with a smoky voice and pinned her against the wall and she fell (or was she pushed?) into love with him. And it was a white Christmas, all covered in snow and the frozen smog of London, when Harry was conceived on some pure snow flown in from Bolivia.

Two decades later, having grown up tall on the immoral high ground, he is standing in his mother's recently decorated corridor, knife in hand, wondering which of the portraits he should slash first.

ALICE

I was feeling a whole lot better since my dealer, a Russian socialite called Valentina, dropped by, and thought it would be fun to go shopping with her. Valentina had an ethereal charm, a way of smiling that made it look like she had secrets and a past she would never tell. She walked, she talked, as if she knew it all, she had it all, she could give you something more. She was so filthy rich, people thought they could trust her not to rip them off. She was so filthy connected that people wouldn't confront her if she did. She could have them all. It was power, but it was also just an act, and Valentina was pretty straightforward really, just went to boarding school like everyone else and looked wealthier than she was. She simply had finesse, had style, and she enjoyed it. She was a true decadent, platinum blonde and sylphlike figure, and she knew how to look exactly how they wanted her to be. It was hopelessly shallow, but it worked, and she was craved all over Kensington.

Valentina happened to have a special affection for me,

said she thought it was cute how I looked so delicate, such a waif, such an innocent, but for the residue of powder under my nose. If that was what she wanted to think. "Let's shop, let's do Harvey Nicks . . ."

We took the elevator up to the women's clothing department, touching the satins and silks and watching the slow glitter of the diamonds . . .

"I love powder, I really do, but I was reading a magazine this morning and discovered to my horror that the drug barons aren't very nice to the Colombian orphans who work for them. Apparently they're starving. I just wish there was a way for everyone to be happy, you know? There must be a way . . .," I was saying, a little high already . . .

"Let them eat coke!" laughed Valentina, and we both started laughing even though it really wasn't that funny at all, walking amidst Versace's neon lighting, laughing for the sake of laughing . . . laughing and laughing, as I started to get anxious again, started to feel intensely guilty, intensely deceived, intensely alone, as my laughter turned to tears and suddenly all I wanted to do was scream . . . and run.

One night I went to a dinner with people I knew from high school, and their parents. It was the third social event of the day and I was tired. We were all tired. We talked and laughed and watched the night fade out fatigued.

The tables were covered in white cloth with small candles flickering in the soft, slow breeze. Pink and white roses stood in vases of glass and the surfaces reflected the candle flames and people swirling by, the girls in a debutante daze. Femininity tended to possess the atmosphere as a nocturne

of natural girlish charm, laughter, sweet nothings and subtle sarcasm flowed with perfumes, scent of ice cream and
champagne. Girls sipped through straws and admired each
other's tans and dresses and shoes. They talked about college next year and vacations, recent breakups, tragedies and
scandals with easy flair and flow. When older people sat at
the table they then talked mostly about anticipation of college and anxiety about finding roommates, often laden with
euphemism.

I started to feel tragic halfway through dinner because
I hated the paradoxes that cut up everything my gaze fell
on. The girls and boys could do just about anything they
wanted and still seem charming and pretty, as if they hardly
touched each other. Partly I was thankful for the communal
lies, as I needed it, but beyond that, I found the falsities
unsettling.

"What are you reading just now?" a lady I had never
met, another girl's aunt, asked me.

"A biography of Zelda Fitzgerald." I replied, "It's so interesting, I've always found her fascinating."

"Yes, I love reading biographies—they're so much better
than a novel or something—I like reading about real people.
You can always find something in their lives that helps you
know what to do—or in the case of Zelda Fitzgerald—what
not to do," and a recognition of notoriety flashed across her
eyes. I smiled politely.

"Where are you going to college next year?"

"I'm taking a year out—I'm taking acting lessons in
London."

"That's so exciting."

"It really is. —Excuse me, I think I'll just go find a
lemonade."

• • •

Sometimes, I found the double act strange, the masquerade where nobody admitted to being crazy but everyone was, where everyone played games and convinced each other of the general façade, the airy foundation of high society. It was all so much foolery, I could see it clearly, but was strangely compelled to keep going.

HARRY

My great-grandfather is in shreds of canvas and paint, his portrait slashed, his image torn down with careless abandon. Because his great-grandson is having a tantrum, a mania, a last stab at the melancholy we share. Depressed, dissatisfied and trapped in gilded frames.

I'm dazed and sick and have no place to go. I slash the portrait of a blonde debutante, then, realizing she looks like Alice, drop the knife and just stare at her broken face. *I murdered her . . . I'm killing myself . . .* glancing at the line of related soldiers and socialites, lying in pieces on the ground . . . *I've killed us all . . .*

No, they're only pictures. They're dead already.

I walk into my mother's bedroom. I pick up her framed photos, smash them on the ground—baby pictures, my father, my parents' wedding—each one until the cream carpet is covered in broken glass, like little diamonds, like little rocks. I move into her bathroom and open her cupboard, and pick out anything that looks like painkillers and put them into my brown leather bag with the knife. I move back through my bedroom, picking up a half-empty bottle of gin on my way out, taking a long swig, and smashing it on the ground with everything else. I have stopped thinking and run on instinct and adrenaline and active fear, an uncontrollable despair, wanting only oblivion, wanting it all gone, every trace of this debauchery, every trace of my corrupt heritage.

I raid the liquor cabinet before getting out of the flat, leaving the door open, walking calmly, heart beating faster, and realizing that it hasn't cured the despair—I don't feel better—I only feel worse, guilty, and alienated. My mother will never forgive me. Which is what I want. I hail a cab to the Marlborough and move into a room there.

● ● ●

Lying back on the bed in my hotel room, my temporary tomb, I feel the rush, my ears ringing. The ringing starts to form words, then I hear a familiar voice:

"Harry, it's been an eternity—what kept you away so long?"

"Has it really been that long?"

"You missed me then?"

"Yes. But you're dead. That's what Leo says."

"I never really died, Harry, you know that . . . I'll always be here . . ."

And I feel the delicate fall of cocaine through my body like a wave—like snow like dirt like stars glittering in their fleeting oblivion. It is something to chase, something to love—the past, it was the future—it's vacant lust for a handful of dust. I'm cutting my silhouette into the surface of life, like footprints in the snow, cutting my life into powder with a knife.

ALICE

I'm in a deep but disturbed daze after feeling sick and strung out all day. I guess I took too much Xanax, and with alcohol, so I've just been lying in bed shaking and feeling sick and feverish. I've been shivering uncontrollably, wondering why it won't stop, drinking lots of water to dilute the pills and alcohol. Then I remembered a story about a friend of a friend who had died after mixing painkillers with alcohol, so I made myself sick. I felt better afterward and subsequently fall into a long slumber, another long nightmare—timeless, because dreams are anarchic in their beat; a sprawling sequence of falls and brawls, fights and trysts—the usual demons . . .

I wake and can't tell the difference between dreams and thoughts.

Because sometimes when I lose control of the depression and I've broken down and cried and died in dreams of suicides, and find I'm still alive . . . Eventually, with mellow moments listening to songs I start to fall into the cloud, and care less and less, and take it all for all it is—fleeting, lonely, compromised. And all I can do is dream and fall and befriend the demons, the voices in my head—shooting myself into fragments, pieces of mind, in hopes I'll find one.

HARRY

I smoke Marlboro Reds and then hash in my hotel room after removing the smoke alarm from the ceiling. I open the window and smoke in the fading breeze. Every way I try to look every particle of light and color breaks into fragments and drains into an abyss. Then a higher light brings me back up again, and then the color and light starts falling, and this circle repeats itself for a couple of hours. Everything pulls me down and betrays me in its facility to fall.

My whole body aches and weakens and I can't see anything but my fall into every direction, every depth, every sphere, direction and place in my mind: the space expands as I breathe through another destruction of another sphere, another belief, another idea. It makes me think of my hands being jammed in a door and being lit on fire, makes me think of being trapped in a sprawling chain and city of animated houses, trapped in an illusion constructed by somebody else. Surroundings stretch and move without my comprehension. Everything drags down and I feel myself diffused into the surrounding mist, and in my mind I want to disintegrate because then it would hurt less. I lie on my bed with my eyes closed.

I turn on the radio and hear music and the music soothes me as I hold on and keep going feeling everything so slow. I feel old and weak, unable to talk or move, only lie with my eyes closed waiting for it all to end. My hands bleed and are lit with flames, and I disintegrate and fade into dust before being reconstructed again and falling again, slow until it usurps me.

After a while I go downstairs into the bar and order a vodka on rocks and think for a while about going to New York and kind of wanting to go but not really caring either way. *Another line? Another pill?*

Skies need clouds of smoke
  And stars of coke

ROSE

I meet Araminta at Liverpool Street station having already bought my ticket, lost my ticket, found my ticket and sipped on a cappuccino. The Victoria Line was screwed so Araminta's also late, but eventually we struggle to the train and find two seats and dump all our bags and stuff and finally sit down. It's ten thirty a.m. and I need a drink already.

Usually vodka in the morning would be a bit wrong but it's a Festival Weekend so it doesn't matter. I buy a cute little bottle of Smirnoff and some Diet Coke and Araminta buys some crisps and we get excited about Latitude.

Some time later, after getting a cab some of the way and traipsing into the campsite we set eyes on our new home: the grass is dry, the sky sublime, and we find a little place near a Ché Guevara flag to pitch our tent.

Only we can't pitch our tent. It's not actually our tent—there are no convenient pictures or instructions. Luckily there are some boys from Sheffield nearby so we ask them to help us. Araminta doesn't want to have to give up, but it's been an hour and the tent is still just some fabric on the ground.

The boys from Sheffield are really good at putting up tents and it's not long before we have a new home, which we quickly leave in pursuit of music and magic.

We buy sangria and walk around in the sunshine. We see colored sheep in the field and the boats on the lake, the Comedy Tent, the Literary Tent, the Beer Tent. After a bit we go to see Jeremy Warmsley play in a tent in the woods and he's brilliant. We sit enraptured and entertained, smoking, talking, swept away by the songs. Afterward we talk to Matt the Drummer briefly who is a friend I once met in a queue for the Magic Numbers by chance, until his tour manager tells him to put everything away. There is apparently a special boat for bands that takes them across the lake, which I'm a bit jealous of. It's the closest you'll get to a yacht in Suffolk.

Araminta and I meanwhile have to walk across the bridge, meeting an awesome music producer called Simon under a big tree. We drink cider and talk about literature and London before straying off to get more cider and watch CSS and get lost in the middle of the crowds, absorbed into an atmosphere something like a Brazilian carnival crossed with a summer's day in Green Park. Spirits are high, Araminta nicks a cowboy hat from some guy and we dance around under blue skies while someone in a pink jumpsuit sings about making love not war.

I'm more excited about the Good, the Bad and the Queen, who are on after CSS just as dusk descends on Henham Park. We move to the front and Araminta's a bit fatigued so she rests on my shoulder while the band take their time . . . Eventually the stage is shrouded in blue and men in top hats with cigarettes saunter into view and set a tone all melancholic and magical as the festival dusk. Their set is languorous and sublime, blasé and beautiful. The images projected onto the stage set and the general dark blue tone casts Victorian airs over the performance, entrancing and addictive, as if the band has just floated out of an opium den or a dusky blues joint.

We later stray into Rodrigo y Gabriella who are really fun and then wander into the wild woods and dance in a little party for a bit, then wander to another part of the woods and meet some boys from Wales who let us share their weed and their daze and we watch the branches dance, sitting in a row on the ground. They're nice boys. When they go off to dance we wander off aimlessly.

We meet another group of boys and sit with them and they let us smoke their weed too. They're from Sheffield and I'm talking to one guy, and he says, "Yeah, we're seeing the Wild Beasts tomorrow—Fred is the drummer," and I say, "Wow, that's such a coincidence—the guys who put up our tent know the Wild Beasts as well . . ."

They give me a look, then one guy says: "WE put up your tent."

"Oh."

Awkward situation, for a minute anyway. I apologize but the damage is done, for a minute anyway.

We talk about Hunter S. Thompson and smoke more weed and look at the trees, talking about the color of the sky and how cool it would be to put hammocks in all the trees and live here forever and ever. "Yeah and like there could be hammocks between every tree—and then we could all just lie there and the trees are close enough that we could just keep passing the joint around . . ."

Araminta disappears and after we have smoked all the weed we go to the Literary Tent because I remember I was going to meet Simon the Producer, and the boys are happy enough to follow.

First we get hot chocolates and teas and then go to the Literary Tent, where there are loads of people. We're not really there for the stories actually, just want to say hi, so we tread carefully through all the people sitting down and say hi to Simon the Producer and he smiles and says, "Shhhh-hhh," because we're not meant to be talking, and then we leave. We walk back across the lake but it takes awhile and the campsite looks like the Yorkshire Moors because of the mist and darkness.

●　●　●

On Sunday I get a burger and cider for breakfast and we hang around in the sunshine for a while before going Speed Dating spontaneously. It's not really Speed Dating though, because there are only two guys there, but they say that's fine and we sit down at little tables and get asked pointless questions and stare into each other's eyes. Araminta sits in a corner for a while, meditating, don't know why.

The Speed Dater, Andrew (blond hair, blue eyes, well of course) is wearing a cute necklace with a pink heart that says "Love Bug" and I tell him I like it. He says, "It's really special to me, but I want to give it to you. But ONLY if you meet me at one thirty a.m. by the big blue elephant," staring deep into my eyes, so I'm like, "Yeah, sure, definitely."

"Do you promise?"

"Sure."

Sadly I can't find a big blue elephant anywhere that night. I think he hallucinated it. The necklace is awesome though.

After that we get our tarot cards read. I get the Lovers, the Sun, the High Priestess, the Emperor and the Fool. This means I'm going to fall in love, be successful and get high apparently. Also, warns the lady, "Watch out for the Law."

Okay.

Araminta and I then meet Matt the Drummer near the crêpe van. Araminta and Matt are both Catholic (I'm just lapsed) so they talk about Catholic school together which is sweet. I realize they look like one another as they both have wavy dark hair, the same almond-shaped eyes and similar lips as well. They don't agree with me though. Matt's wearing a straw hat and a wife-beater and Araminta's wearing the straw hat she nicked during CSS yesterday and I'm wearing a black trilby I just bought. Matt says it's all about the hats. After much cider and banter we go to the theater and see one play I really like and one I really don't.

After this we go to see the Rapture who are sunny though we're not paying that much attention I must confess. We meet some people who Matt knows and then get some food. I have a food fight with Luke the Drummer and get smeared with chocolate sauce so I make sure Luke gets covered in it too. Then we go to see Arcade Fire and they're amazing. We drink we dance we smoke we sing . . . It's beautiful and for a moment it rains and then stops when the singer prays to God to stop it raining or whatever, I'm not sure exactly what he did and said but it worked. There are fireworks and more dancing and everyone's happy, and then it's all over so suddenly, which seems unfair somehow.

Matt and the rest of Jeremy's band have to leave, so Araminta and I go off with an actress and her fun boyfriend to hang out backstage. We only have one extra pass though and although Araminta and I hold hands and smile sweetly at the security man, and then start running when he refuses us entry, it all goes wrong and Araminta gets manhandled and only I manage to get backstage. I talk to an Irish actor who buys me some vodka and we chill out at the Pink Flamingo on pink chairs and under a disco ball. Araminta meanwhile is getting more passes from Jeremy's band and eventually gets back in so all is good. Before Araminta gets back I chat with Elmo (the boyfriend of the actress) about hallucinogenics and films and stuff, and we notice the weird scene we're on the edge of: burlesque people, a girl dressed as a cat, another as a sort of sexy version of the bunny from *Donnie Darko*, dancing together with a weird short Chinese belly dancer who really annoys us.

Then Araminta appears and we talk and we dance and the cider is chemical-tasting by this stage so I drink vodka instead and we talk and we dance and we drink and we smoke and we dance and . . .

HARRY

The harsh light of an unusually bright morning wakes me from a stoned slumber too early for it to feel natural. I lie around for a bit before ordering room service because I haven't eaten in a few days and the room keeps sliding every time I try to get up. And I've been dwelling on the tragedy of my life like an idiot while feeling guilty for being destructive... Guilty about Alice . . . and I take the tray from the waiter, because I don't want him to come in and smell the hash, pick it up feeling miserable and hungover, and try as best as I can to put it carefully on the bed. I don't feel very hungry and don't want to eat, but make myself because I'm about to pass out. I eat some toast and drink the coffee but can't face the eggs because they make me feel nauseous. I sip some orange juice and think that something about it doesn't taste right, then realize the vodka's missing, but there's nothing I can do because I already drank everything in the minibar.

ALICE

I leave my room early in the morning because my father came home again and I don't want to be anywhere near him. He has a violent kind of presence. He's always angry, and there is a sort of habitual threat that any moment he'll snap . . . Sometimes he's gone for weeks. But he's never really far away. His presence leaves a stale scent of anger behind him. I have nightmares sometimes where he shouts at me and hits me, so that even when he's away, his smoky presence hangs in the air.

It's strange, because I was shy when I was younger. And now I've lost my reserve, my inhibition. When I feel like complaining, I complain. When I feel sad, I cry hard. When I want a joint, I smoke a joint. And once I had fallen into that mentality, I couldn't stop. I always saw it as taking care of myself, of taking control or losing control, depending on the day's whim. If I wanted life to be more fun, I'd buy a little bag of cocaine, I'd fly to New York, I'd go to a fashion show. Nothing was too much, nothing was enough, nothing was even close.

So I walk fast through the streets, all vacant because it is raining so hard, and walk without any direction but farther and farther away. Something in the wet, colder air shakes me up, wakes me up, sobers me up . . . Suddenly I'm straight, level, balanced, as if waking from a dream, my personal Wonderland, my Wasteland, a little of both in a handful of dust.

The clouds have shifted, the sky is pale but bright. For the first time in months I feel awake. And I can't stand it anymore.

HARRY

I throw the phone at the wall because I don't want to speak to anyone and lie back, the room still spinning, my thoughts giving me a kind of nausea, the way they don't match, don't fit, aren't synchronized, don't stream . . .

Distractions of abstractions . . . game playing to confuse genuine attraction, hostile affections that are no more than friendly affections, the pointless labyrinth of fleeting seductions. All that is the pulp. I can't tell the difference between heaven and hell anyway . . .

There is rubble everywhere, so all we can do is look around, salvage the values that remain—though I forget what they are—in a few words exchanged now and again, a few songs, a few moments of clarity—and use them to build something new, though I can't think what . . . And of course the houses keep falling down again, but the original materials will always remain somehow. And though the physique will change and reality turns to pulp so quickly, and provokes pulp reactions from confused people who can see clearly that events are in pieces and go to pieces with them as people dancing react to music . . .

So I keep looking for something higher, keep living a pulp reality, looking for the real amidst the fallacy and driven by nothing but a taste for substance clear and lofty as gin poured into a white china teacup, and a meantime addiction to the fiction I am raking through.

ALICE

I walk very slowly and carefully through Harrods, a little nervous of the crowds, but feeling so happy, so soon, so quick, more painkillers and alcohol, champagne this time. The bartender is so encouraging.

"I'm not sure," I say, "I probably shouldn't have another flute of champagne, it's only eleven a.m. after all," and he laughs and replies, "But it's never too early for champagne," and I can't help but agree. Never too early for pills, either . . . So I drink more Moët, falling into my soft little cloud, my happiness the color of pink champagne, my high the sound of a love song, my euphoria the scent of roses and champagne, that dragging scent, that amorous gaze, that falling into the sheets and falling far below.

My phone rings a few too many times and I just ignore it, as I float and flirt with the bartender and flit around with every care diffused into the cloud and turned to something pretty. And two flutes of champagne isn't really enough either, because it should never have to fade, so a whole orchestra of flutes of champagne is required for me to get through the morning.

So I walk through the departments and see through the people and wander around the shop not seeing anything I want all that much really, wondering if maybe Harvey Nicks could tempt me . . . Wondering if maybe one more trip to the bar would tempt me, knowing that it would, wanting it to—caring less and less about Harry or anyone else, feeling a melody playing up in my soul, an indulgent little blues song, a soft little harmony, a careless little opiate reverie . . . Remembering Harry's songs, how he played them for me, and drifting back through all the confusion to that night, those nights, of guitar and crowds, and vodka and Harry, under the blur, thoughts and feelings asunder, lying on the ground. Falling in a dream . . . I become aware that my hair is all disheveled and wonder if I should get a haircut, but lose interest as soon as I smell a perfume that reminds me of something, someone . . . Rosé . . . and suddenly I want Rosé to come shopping also, but then realize Rosé is being boring presently, all those lessons she wants to teach—but school was out years ago.

I go into the elevator and press all the buttons, but don't get out until the top floor, where I get out and try to find a window, to see the habitat of my habit, the smoke, the buildings touching clouds, the sky, the lies, the scrapers, the pictures in the papers . . . I find one building to look at, and fixate my gaze on one window millions of miles away and wonder if someone in that window is looking over in my direction, thinking it is pretty to think about . . . I leave and take the elevator way back down again and drift toward the little smoking boutique—the cigars, lighters, fire, smoke—and I buy another lighter, something more to set the world alight, this time zebra-print, to coordinate with my outfit . . . Buy some cherry cloves, some vanilla cloves, opening the packets as soon as I've paid to smell the vanilla mixed with tobacco, suddenly dying for a drag . . . So I walk out of the shop and sit on a stone wall and light up a vanilla clove and remember I used to smoke these all the time, in New York, in Connecticut, and wondering why I forgot about them. They left a sugary aftertaste . . . *Why do I always forget that this is it? This is all.*

The rain clears and it is a pretty enough day . . . after smoking the vanilla cigarettes, I think that maybe I should find another bar, chase another oblivion, as my head begins to hurt again, and I am beginning to feel sad again, and the memories are returning again . . . and Harrods is shit, I realize, why did I come here . . . And at once there is nothing else I want to do, no higher desire—and nowhere to go. There is nothing to chase, and no way to escape the fears and depression that chase me . . . Always chasing, in every oblivion and in every dream of every day, something is chasing me—that clock, that cloud, that Wonderland, that dream: *Off with her head . . .*

HARRY

I'm off my head and lying in bed, the time flickering by slower than I want, feeling sad and mad, all alone in the zone . . . Two more lines and then it is all gone, I'm all gone, wired for a bit, then sadder than before, pulled down by my own overwhelming gravity. I walk into the bathroom and notice my reflection in the mirror, pale and strung out: *I thought you were dead . . .* I think.

"I never really died," I hear myself say . . .

Things rapidly start falling into place, my mind skipping forward like a broken record:

"I never really died—I shifted into another sphere, that's all . . . I'm not dead, I'm not dead . . ."—the record skipping back—

"I never really died—I shifted into another sphere, that's all . . . I'm not dead, I'm not dead . . ."—the record skipping back—

"I never really died—I shifted into another sphere, that's all . . . I'm not dead, I'm not dead . . ."

I watch how my lips are moving unwittingly, speaking these words I have heard before . . . Heard from that strung-out man who haunts me, possessing the clouds, changing the clocks, melting the rocks and burning London for its big smoke . . .

That pale and strung-out face is now my own: *Was my father ever here? Was that me all along? Or have I turned into him. . . ?*

"I never really died," I say to myself: "I just grew up . . . I just grew into you."

I look at this reflection: what I have grown up into: an image of my father, a distortion of my previous self, a new reality.

"*Reality is a flexible thing. We can defy it. We can change it—we can determine the future . . .*"

And I have determined my own future, I have altered my landscape, my image, have painted in myself a portrait of my dead father and become it.

The image possesses me.

"I thought you were dead . . ." I ask myself.

"I never really died—I shifted into another sphere, that's all . . . I'm not dead, I'm not dead . . .," I reply to myself.

And so I'm falling into the smoky gray eyes of myself, feeling faint as a cloud . . .

"*There are many possible realities, dimensions, whatever you want to call it—there are so many different ways, Harry. Some ways are better than others . . . You know that. You know that figments of your imagination make more sense than a sober traipse down through this city . . .*"

"Revenge on reality?"

Yes.

"How?"

You're almost there now . . .

I walk back into the room, shutting my itching eyes and collapsing on the bed, not my own bed, never my own bed these days.

I imagine my mother returning home to the scene—like some war zone, a hall of socialites and soldiers knocked down in a massacre of pictures of her past. She steps carefully through the carpet of remnants of reminiscence, knowing the culprit to be me, moving by ingrained instinct into the drawing room and her drinks cabinet—only to find that all her other friends—gin, tonic, and champagne—have also fallen. So she falls with them—one more figure sprawled wrecked on the dark blue carpet, fallen in a wasteland of dukes and earls and wine and pearls, Krug and girls sad-eyed with gin.

ALICE

So I turn off my phone and walk into my favorite club, which has a pool that I really need right now, because my head is aching worse than it has in a long time, realizing that the moment of clarity was only that—a moment—and here is the further stream of sensation—a head aching from my eyes through my skull down my neck down my spine, making each step painful.

I put my Chanel sunglasses on though there is no real sun, only a vapid screaming brightness bearing down on me from the sky. I keep walking, feeling sort of blind, not watching, not looking, ignoring every other person in the street, along Piccadilly, realizing I'm not one of them, or *one of us*, as my father always says in the same pretentious tone . . . I'm not one of anything much anymore. I'm one more name on a guest list every other day, but the novelty has worn thin and the privilege doesn't excite me anymore. The further I get into the center, the further away I get from my own center, shooting to the moon, getting lost and floating.

• • •

Is it worth it? Probably—but that doesn't make the end any easier, doesn't explain the comedown, doesn't explain why all that lifts off must fall down to the depths. And it doesn't make the waking hour easier, and it doesn't make Harry appear except in distorted images in disturbed dreams and a slow disillusionment with faith in the thrill of the moment . . .

Each thrilling moment killing the next moment in advance.

Swallow another pill and keep walking, straight through to the bar on the third floor of the club, a couple double vodka cranberries, immediately easing the pain raging, then blurring the cityscape out the window, far off, too far, and then it's time to go, and the hearts and diamonds won't appear anymore . . . I trip but nobody secs, and I walk straight, seeing it all dimmed and hazy in the artificial light of a dark hallway . . . I walk into a changing room, lock it and sit down, head down, slumped against the wall, slumped against the edge, pushing indifferently into another side . . . What's on the other side?

I breathe deeply but it feels shallow and I stand up and it spins like it mostly does these days, these sways, this haze, this daze . . . and I steady myself and strip, wanting a cigarette, hating that fucking ban, and change into a silver bikini I bought for Ibiza. I take the bottle of pills and one by one swallow each one with Evian and I leave the changing room, too hot, then shivering . . . And I stand over the edge of the pool and briefly see my reflection in the mirrors everywhere as I fall in one more time, plunge into the water, not feeling any cold because I'm all so numb, gradually, closing my eyes and feeling free as I fall the same as in every one of

those dreams, but undisturbed, no voices, no one anywhere
. . . Only the soft serenity of my slumber, only the sorrows
drowning, only the asphyxiation I try to ignore, the sudden
choking as I scream one more time, but nobody can hear me,
and what did I expect anyway? The thoughts rush my mind
suddenly and then in the next moment everything breaks
and ends with fading beats. I feel my mind shut down. I cannot move and lie paralyzed, in a dull, aching despair, falling
once more into the dream I can't ever escape.

I've spent all of this time trying to find a way and find
myself—only to know in one sweeping sensation, lying in
shadows in water, looking down upon myself . . . that I had
achieved nothing except losing myself. I feel my mind giving
up, fading out. I feel my soul drift away. I break as whatever is left—physical sensations and memories—fade and
fall into blue despair, disappear into my dream, scatter like
shards of glass, rocks, diamonds, ash, pretending to be stars
in the sky.

HARRY

And I'm getting scared by the voices in my head—my voice, strange words—so I head down to the bar, the Homage, ignoring everyone else, looking beat, order a vodka, neat . . . shadows beating out some bass line—I want just one more base white line, my sweet decline, reality's roguish rhyme . . .

I hold up the neat vodka to the domineering cloud of light: raging spite, falling from that height—in homage to my father, in the right bar, in the wrong light.

Drowning in a shot glass . . . amplifying the voices in my head, this time Alice . . . *Through the Shot Glass, I was Looking, saw my distorted reflection, astray perfection, by your dejection . . . your false rejection, your lost erection, your low selection, of priority . . . You were my run away, my rogue distraction . . .*

I knock back another vodka, this time on rocks, cooling my chiding throat, my burning broken heart.

• • •

I stay in the bar all afternoon, at last clambering back to my room around six thirty, the alcohol no longer doing much for me but causing one more stream of depression . . . Something a little stronger is in order. I think about how convenient it would be if room service provided cocaine . . . Wondering if there was a way . . . *Probably* . . . But no way I know anything about.

I call Patrick, therefore, and arrange to meet him in the bar in roughly an hour. I throw my phone on the floor again, wondering why, no matter how hard I throw it, or how many times I throw it—it doesn't break.

Although it's difficult to walk, I go and retrieve it, just to test my theory that it's invincible . . . Only to find that this time it is broken, turned off, screen blank. And I can't help but feel that the blank dark screen is some sort of omen, some sort of sign, even if that does sound paranoid . . . Smashing it against the wall again, I put my head in my hands, my eyes itching, my skin crawling, tears burning down my face and heart beating beats all astray. *I should have stopped this so long, long ago, the spiders are itching away at my soul* . . . I look at the ceiling and see a spider, and then another and then another and the words melt into my mind: *watched, chased, killed, traced, drinks laced with poison and London a trick, a treat*, and it repeats in my mind over and over again, finding it comforting, in some small way, to hear my own voice in my head . . .

I should have stopped this so long, long ago, the spiders are itching away at my soul . . . watched, chased, killed, traced, drinks laced with poison and London a trick, a treat . . . I should have stopped this so long, long ago, the spiders are itching away at my soul . . . watched, chased, killed, traced,

drinks laced with poison and London a trick, a treat . . . I
should have stopped this so long, long ago, the spiders are
itching away at my soul . . . watched, chased, killed, traced,
drinks laced with poison and London a trick, a treat . . . I
should have stopped this so long, long ago, the spiders are
itching away at my soul . . . watched, chased, killed, traced,
drinks laced with poison and London a trick, a treat . . . I
should have stopped this so long, long ago, the spiders are
itching away at my soul . . . watched, chased, killed, traced,
drinks laced with poison and London a trick, a treat . . . I
should have stopped this so long, long ago, the spiders are
itching away at my soul . . . watched, chased, killed, traced,
drinks laced with poison and London a trick, a treat . . . I
should have stopped this so long, long ago, the spiders are
itching away at my soul . . . watched, chased, killed, traced,
drinks laced with poison and London a trick, a treat . . . I
should have stopped this so long, long ago, the spiders are
itching away at my soul . . . watched, chased, killed, traced,
drinks laced with poison and London a trick, a treat . . . I
should have stopped this so long, long ago, the spiders are
itching away at my soul . . . watched, chased, killed, traced,
drinks laced with poison and London a trick, a treat . . . I
should have stopped this so long, long ago, the spiders are
itching away at my soul . . . watched, chased, killed, traced,
drinks laced with poison and London a trick, a treat . . . I
should have stopped this so long, long ago, the spiders are
itching away at my soul . . . watched, chased, killed, traced,
drinks laced with poison and London a trick, a treat . . . I
should have stopped this so long, long ago, the spiders are
itching away at my soul . . . watched, chased, killed, traced,
drinks laced with poison and London a trick, a treat . . .
I should have stopped this so long, long ago, the spiders
are itching away at my soul . . . watched, chased, killed,
traced, drinks laced with poison and London a trick, a treat.
I should have stopped

HUGO

Alice left me some day in February, when winter was dragging its heels and she was being careless but I still loved her in some addicted way. I was back in London after working in New York for a couple months, and invited her, my on and off and here and there girlfriend, for dinner. I hadn't seen her in more than a month, because she had returned home in November when she began to romanticize London once again. Maybe she wanted a change, a flight, another distraction. I don't, never really do, never really will, understand her . . .

It takes me too, that diversion, that dust storm of giddy highs and forgotten lows.

I called her up and proposed a date. I took her to the Bellini Bar at Hospital for a drink first. This choice of venue nearly swayed her back in the direction of a relationship, I could tell, the way she was looking at the pretty people and pretty décor and patterns on the wall, some elaborate graffiti by Soho sellouts.

She sipped a strawberry bellini and looked as if she was about to cry like the little child that she sometimes was.

"Alice, what's wrong? Don't you like it here?"

"No, I love it."

"Then why the tragic face?"

Alice paused, looking around, looking at the intricate patterns on the wall, the intense blue tone, the pretty people.

"Hugo, I can't stand having to tell you this. But it's been forever since we were last together, and in that huge time lapse—I found someone else."

"We were together a couple months ago. I can't believe this."

"I'm sorry, Hugo."

I didn't speak, just downed my Jack Daniel's and ordered another.

"Who?"

Alice looked timid and finished her bellini, "Harry Law."

"The son of Charlie Law?" I asked.

"You know him?"

"Yes. You just shouldn't be involved."

"You're involved."

"That's different," I say.

"I doubt that very much."

"He is different . . . Look, it doesn't matter."

"It does matter, Alice, it matters to me." I ordered her another bellini and myself another Jack Daniel's. "I know I haven't been around much recently, but I think of you all the time. Harry's obviously just a fling. It's not serious, it's not real. How old is he?"

"Nineteen."

I paused, feeling old, downing my Jack Daniel's . . . "Well he's too young for you. He won't be able to look after you."

"I don't need looking after, Hugo, I can look after myself. I'm sorry." With that, she downed her bellini and left, running away before she gave herself the chance to change her mind. Maybe she had reasons to run. It didn't look like she could remember them though.

So I never really got over her, even if she got over me. Although I played around a bit, found my older woman, left my older woman, got high in Ibiza and low in rehab, I couldn't find another relationship that I was comfortable with. After the initial high of being out of rehab and back in the big, bad city, I was tired, so so fucking tired, of playing around, getting around, flying from place to place. Only it looked like Alice was not. I think in wanting her I merely wanted to be like her again, as I had been in my youth, which left me when she left me too.

When I came back from rehab and met Alice in Sketch, despite all the insolence and argument, I convinced myself that the tension was sexual rather than spite alone, and convinced myself that she was on the verge of leaving Harry.

I had previously met Alice's father, Frank, when she and I were still together, and we liked each other, we had all these connections—cousins who went to the same schools, friends who lived in the same bars, business along the same lines. Then we met again the end of summer. Both of us agreed that Harry was just a wasted youth, stringing Alice along in a hotel room kind of relationship—temporary, fleeting, superficial . . . And sooner or later, Alice was going to tire of living in hotel rooms. Everyone has to settle sooner or later. And although Alice was young, she'd been so unsettled for so long that maybe settling down was what she needed. It was what I needed anyway. I kept forgetting she was barely out of school.

● ● ●

When Frank calls me it is six thirty, and I'm relaxing in my club in Covent Garden with an old friend from Charterhouse. I pick up his call, Long Island Iced Tea in hand, to hear Frank's weak voice:

"I should tell you this in person, I know, but I'm in no state to see anybody right now. Alice nearly drowned today, Hugo. She overdosed and then she fell into a pool . . ." His voice trails off and I put my drink down, walking fast out of the crowded bar. "Frank, how did this happen? Why?"

Frank doesn't reply for a while. I hear a sigh, then he continues: "I have no idea. It's happened so suddenly . . . I can't help but think—I know it sounds awful—but I can't help thinking that ever since she started dating Harry Law she's become more and more distant. I can't help but think that he had something to do with this."

"I'll sort it out, Frank. Speak soon," and I hang up.

As it is the Hospital, I take a little medication to distract my shock, the substance on call all through the evening and night . . . My only stability, my only break, the only constant thing in a life of fleeting breaking abstractions: Alice, cocaine—love, war—fire, ice.

HARRY

I've been pacing my hotel room for the previous two hours, eyes too sore to keep open, but unable to close them because I'm too restless, too scared of the dark.

I order up a coffee at seven, and a glass of gin.

I take a shower, shivering under the hot water, crying with the cold.

Light up a cigarette, then another, then another, until even my cigarettes are gone. After that I play with my lighter, watching the flame flicker, wane, blowing it out and lighting matchsticks, dreaming about arson halfheartedly. Sad really, that I play with my lighter when I used to play a guitar.

HUGO

I play with the fire of my lighter in the taxi—the driver oblivious to the little sparks of light flickering in the dark, reflections lit on black faux leather, the dirty windows and my eyes burn, my visions all askew. It's still so light outside—people sprawling all over central London. Such an old city, such a long Blitz, such stale smoke . . . such fresh fire . . . such unrequited desires . . . It was a bad lie, but such a good time (in a white line).

I remembered the white sands of Ibiza, the sun beating down and everything gone—in an everything goes kind of place—everything gone but the white sand falling through my fingers as I sat on the beach and felt so alone. There were only brief encounters and friends who were really just acquaintances, and no connections that meant anything after the highs wore off, only me all worn down and lost. That was when I decided to get Alice back, decided to get myself, my mind back, from all the trappings of decadence I succumbed to, so easily. Too easily.

But not much time of relative purity passed and the white sands returned, little beaches of lies. And Ibiza was never very far away, my escape was only a three-hour flight, or a phone call, or a trip to another stall—only I could never find what I wanted to find, and begin to think, as I imagine Alice drowned, washed up on the white sands of some Neverland—that perhaps I never, never will. When I first enter the hospital I'm not allowed to see Alice because she's in Intensive Care and I'm not family. I tell them she's my fiancée but they don't believe me, perhaps I look too old.

It's a bad time for a comedown. I start shouting at the receptionist and then the doctor and the nurses and then I knock over a wheelchair and a trolley, and then Security restrain me, and I start crying, everyone in the E.R. is looking at me like I'm insane, like I've lost my mind, like I'm dangerous, like I'm having a really bad midlife crisis, seeing straight through me the way only strangers can. I open my eyes and the first person I see is a little girl, about eight, with blonde hair and big eyes, and she looks terrified. I stop crying. I say, "I'm sorry, Alice, I'm sorry . . ." And I keep repeating it and start crying again, and the little girl starts crying and her alarmed mother picks her up and takes her away, and Security take me away. I can't stop crying. I ask for a doctor and although it isn't protocol someone comes and sees me and asks me why I lashed out and all at once it comes spilling out, that I can't cope anymore, that I have been taking too much cocaine for too many years and life itself had usurped me . . . I have been destroying other people's lives. I need help.

HARRY

The Wrecking Ball

I'm feeling a bit better after I took some Valium and fell asleep for sixteen hours. I dreamt a succession of objects askew in the purple sky—no ground, no meaning, no past no present.

A glass of red wine.

Red lips.

A black plate.

A red knife.

Big black sunglasses.

Pin-prick pupils.

The silhouette of a girl's darkened figure sleeping.

By the time I wake up my bank account is empty, my soul is rushing toward bankruptcy. These images in my mind mean little to me but haunt me still. I draw them on hotel room paper, the lines joining them, the red wine flowing from the girl's heart, the red knife piercing the dark glasses, looking for a pupil, looking for a focus. The images, attached together, look better than as previously askew. And somehow, though I can't articulate any meaning, the picture expresses some violent problem blinding my visions and casting vapid sweet nothings where reality should have been.

• • •

"Come to the Wrecking Ball, Harry, I haven't seen you in weeks, where have you been?" Leo has no tone in his voice. But he draws me in anyway.

"I can't remember."

"Sounds bad." I can hear him drag on his cigarette or spliff or whatever before continuing, "Well tonight will be a night to remember."

Leo persuades me to go to his sister's party in some field in Suffolk. I don't really want to go because I'm so bummed out but I go anyway because I need some human contact.

ALICE

The first thought I have upon waking is that I want Harry.

Well of course he isn't here. My suspicions are confirmed. Of course he doesn't love me. It was lovely in the beginning though, and therefore hard to believe that all that passion could be so diluted by ennui.

In the beginning it had all felt genuine, but as time went on things revealed themselves to be delusions, our relationship turned old, I got bored and desperate and Harry got sick of it.

It was getting boring and repetitive, the whole thing. It's probably why I took the plunge—I just felt the desire to clear my mind, once and for all. Though I must confess it was a relief to wake up again. I didn't really want to die. I just wanted to flirt with the edge. I wanted the pain gone for a while.

• • •

When I wake I realize I need more than a temporary cure, a lonely plateau. I need a life, a future, some integrity of my own to hold on to.

I don't want to race against a lover anymore. I don't want sweet nothings and white lies. I don't want a meaningless dance where we all fall down. I want harmony and space. I want to have faith in a future rather than lust for a fleeting life of ephemeral sensations. I want the lust to mean something. I want it to mean love.

So my second thought upon waking, after, "Where is Harry?" is not, "Where is my vodka?" or "Where are the narcotics?" . . . It is a question that is harder to ask, because it is harder to get.

"Where is my stage?"

"Where is my script?"

HARRY

Where's Alice?"

Leo looks at me with his dead eyes, then speaks in mocking voice:

"The girl's sick, mate."

He drags some more on his spliff, sitting on the faded green grass and sweating in the late afternoon heat. It sticks to his gaunt face, the end of summer.

"What do you mean?"

"Well the story goes she tried to top herself. OD'd and then fell into a pool apparently. I don't know the details, but a girl I used to know told me she was a heroin addict and her parents found out and cut her allowance and she couldn't deal with the withdrawal so she OD'd on like pills or something cheap and then she nearly drowned. Apparently."

"Bullshit."

ROSE

When I get to Maya's party, the Wrecking Ball, I'm feeling exhausted. Alice is being aloof and I can't get through to Harry or Leo or anyone. I feel cut off. I don't feel myself. And perhaps I am feeling bad about losing my job, and perhaps I am feeling sick and tired and confused, a failure, a fake, and perhaps it is getting late.

And yet the sun refuses to set: it is only four p.m.

HARRY

I don't understand why Leo is lying to me and start getting angry with him until he gives me some pills and then everything just feels better. No pain, no game—but I hate the game—but I am a player—but I don't want to be—No Pain . . .

Rose appears sometime and we share some more pills with her and although I am trying not to think about Alice and all these crazy stories she brings her up again, she says, "Where's Alice? I haven't seen her in days, she won't pick up, she won't pick up when I call," but I have no answer, no reply, and I can't pick up.

But I do anyway.

"Got coke?"

ROSE

No, maybe Leo found some by now."

Harry doesn't speak, he nods, then leads the way, weaving through the emaciated inebriated crowds, the hollow rapture, the pain and emptiness of not knowing where to go or who to know, of needing simply more.

I hold his hand as we walk faster and see Leo and then we run.

HARRY

And Leo hasn't got any drugs and I can't deal with this anymore and we keep running, keep running farther away, running circles round some field in England somewhere green, somewhere dark, somewhere dank, somewhere new, somewhere old. We keep running and running until I can't go on and fall to the ground far away from the crowds, music pumping dead in the distance, my other heartbeat, beating fast, beating slow, my heart is base, a bass guitar, my soul is low.

ROSE

I can't see anything because it is so dark and my glow stick is ineffective. I can't see Harry anywhere. I start calling, he doesn't answer. I start shouting but he isn't there, and I can't understand where he has gone, because there is nowhere to go. But down.

Everyone has left me. I can't get an answer from anyone, not even myself. They aren't picking up. I can't talk, can't walk, can't feel, can't think. I can only cry this time, and wonder vaguely—why?

HARRY

I dream a succession of objects askew in the purple sky—
no ground, no meaning, no past, no present.
 A glass of red wine.
 Red lips.
 A black plate.
 A red knife.
 Big black sunglasses.
 Pin-prick pupils.
 The silhouette of a girl's darkened figure sleeping.

"Rose . . . Rose?"
 She doesn't wake up.
 Rose is sick. I'm beat and blue.
 My life, our lives: defeat: askew.

ROSE

So how was the Wrecking Ball?"

"I can't remember," I reply.

"Was it that bad?"

"It may have been great, I just don't know."

"Wake up, sweetie. I'll buy you lunch."

I haven't eaten a decent meal in a while and despite the constant sense of nausea that now grips me after whatever caused me to forget a couple days of my life, I follow Marina to a little place in Soho and rest my head on her shoulder as we wait for salad and steak.

"What's wrong, darling?" she says, sipping on a lemonade, fresh-faced and pretty.

"I don't know."

"You can tell me, sweetie, really, I won't tell anyone anything at all."

"I know. But seriously—I just don't know—what happened."

• • •

The food arrives and I realize suddenly that I'm starving and eat the whole meal. Then I feel much better.

"That was so good."

"Rose, why are you so vapid? You don't seem yourself at all. You're all—down. You're usually so—up . . ."

"I think I'm just tired."

"When was the last time you slept?"

"Well I slept all week—on and off—but I didn't sleep very well because I was sleeping in a field and on a floor. I'm just tired of it all."

"Well maybe you should just take a break from all the partying. Because otherwise you'll end up like Alice."

"What do you mean?"

Marina puts her lemonade down. "Babes, haven't you heard?"

I signal a No.

Marina sighs. Her tone drops to a poignant secretive whisper.

"She nearly fucking died—that's what happened."

Wednesday, July 25

HARRY

You could have died, Harry." My mother is standing in front of a ripped canvas of some ancestor. I know I'm wrong but I can't stop hating her.

"Stop lecturing me. Stop telling me what to do, I hate you."

"Don't speak to me like that. I've been through hell with you. First you insult me, then you wreck my flat, then you nearly die in a field in Suffolk. I've had enough, Harry. It's gone too far."

"If it's gone too far then why do I feel so bored. Why am I so trapped?"

"I don't know, Harry. But I gave you space, I gave you freedom. You have to take responsibility for yourself, you can't keep blaming me."

"I'm not listening to this."

"If you won't listen to me then perhaps you'll listen to someone else. Maybe you need to talk to someone else about losing your father, maybe you need someone else, maybe you need help, Harry."

"Fuck off."

"I've booked you into rehab. The cab's waiting."

I run. Run, run, run . . .

Friday, July 27

ROSE

I was just walking slow down Dean Street, beat and confused about Alice, not wanting to believe in the things I had heard, when I heard a beautiful tune. I looked up and a band was practicing in the flat above where Push Bar used to be, a window open and the tune playing down into the street. I stopped and leaned against the wall opposite the building, lit up a cigarette and listened for a while. I really loved it.

By chance the guitarist playing by the window caught my eye and I waved back and then thought why not, and went and rang the doorbell so I could listen some more. I was expecting it to be some random boy I'd never met before, so when the door opened and it was two boys I knew from Scotland, whom I'd met a few months ago at a friend's house, I gasped with surprise, as did they. I explained the whole thing to them, "I had no idea it was you, I just thought your songs were amazing," so they led me inside and upstairs where they were practicing.

I sat down and lit up another cigarette and met the other guy in the band and also the guys who owned the flat. It was the most ideal place. There were books, I can't remember which ones but at the time I liked them, and a bar disguised as a globe, and ashtrays and wine everywhere . . . We talked a bit and I told them about my weird day.

"Well first I couldn't focus on anything because I only slept three hours last night. And then I was in a lingerie shop on Old Compton Street when I got a call from Johnny Borrell asking me for his leather jacket back, which I accidentally nicked from him one cold morning after his party" (because baby, it was cold outside), "And he said, Where are you? So I replied, Well I'm in a lingerie shop actually, so he told me to meet him in Groucho's which was close. So I went to Groucho's and sat around and Johnny was taking his time. Eventually he rolled up on his motorbike and I gave it back to him saying it looked way better on him than me, though I must confess I had grown quite attached to it, and he was like yeah, it's brand new, I just broke it in, and then I kissed him good-bye and he rode off and I went back to work."

Max, the vocalist and guitarist, still couldn't get over how weird this random and yet fated meeting was . . . They were playing their first gig that very night at eight p.m. So I phoned Bella and she said she'd come along, and of course in the end it was wonderful, they played so well, shambolic as late August, all of us crammed into a little flat and the tunes making me happy, clouds of cigarette smoke and little flames, dancing and sitting and eyes glittering as it poured with rain outside in Soho. We went up onto the rooftop anyway, all dark now and inky amber lights, glancing at the cityscape of flats and offices and studios surrounding, stars shining and rain thundering down, and then we went to Camden . . .

I met Alice there, sipping on a vodka cranberry and smoking a cigarette under an umbrella outside in the rain. I hadn't seen or spoken to her since we argued a couple weeks ago or whenever it was. I had missed her. Our fights never broke us up though, so I went and spoke to her.

"Don't spit on me, England," she said aloud, little raindrops diluting her vodka.

"Alice, how are you? I've missed you so much."

"I'm fine."

"Cool, because there have been all these stories, but I didn't believe them. I tried to call but you wouldn't pick up. I don't know what happened, but it's all been crazy and—how are you?"

"I'm fine, really. But this place bores me, I'm leaving soon."

"Where are you going?"

"Not sure."

She turned away and I realized I couldn't connect and her eyes, as she rejected my gaze, said nothing more to me than Leave Me Alone.

She started talking to someone else. I sipped my vodka tonic. I felt so sick. I wanted to go home but I couldn't remember where it was.

I watched the crowds shift and wished I could merge and be happy, but the pills didn't last forever.

Eternity only entertained for an evening.

HARRY

I had known for some time that Alice and I had no future together if things carried on as they did: wrecked and falling further: but when I heard she nearly drowned I realized seriously for the first time that there is an edge that we had both been running toward blindly in the absurd delusion that one or other of us would break the fall. We were guitar and drums, and the rhythm slipped with the tune, and the song fell apart.

She fell first but it could easily have been me. In many ways I had died again and again. And yet there's something about drugs that gives an amnesiac aftertaste. I would sink into a depressed plateau for hours and days and while on that plateau I'd swear to myself never to do it again, never to put myself into that paralyzed position. But then I'd come round and feel high from just feeling again, telling myself that it had been the catharsis I needed to free my mind, and then only a few hours later someone would offer me some more ketamine or methadone or painkillers and I'd say yes, why not, I'm bored, I'm depressed, and fall one more time.

When Alice fell too far the pursuit of blissful ignorance began to fall to pieces and I saw it all for the pointless sham that it was and it is. I felt suddenly so sad that we had lost all that time just losing our minds.

My father and the way he lived his life had been haunting me and taunting me, and I wanted it to end. He ran away from my mother and me when he ran away with drugs—his mistress and his murderer. Now that same force beckons me into a false embrace, a hollow desire, and a loveless affair. I can see how pointless it is but I'm seduced all the same. I can try to resist though. I can try to leave. Music is a better lover.

ROSE

E ternity's evening sets. Vague plans disintegrate.
Then the rigid morning comes, down.

And although in many ways we had already hit rock bottom, nevertheless it spiraled further into chaos, our lives,
because we drifted apart, Alice, Harry and I. The picnics on
Hampstead Heath years ago felt suddenly so impossibly past,
so gone. The present nausea was inescapable. We mirrored
each other's descent too clearly for it to feel comfortable,
for us to stay together, for now anyway. There was something perverse in how we had let one another self-destruct.
It made me wonder if in fact we destroyed ourselves—or if
really we destroyed one another.

Each of us, after the Wrecking Ball in Suffolk and Alice
nearly drowning—after we all ended up in hospital with water on the lungs and kidney infections and general malaise—
after that we each tried to run our separate routes through
the impossible labyrinth. Each of us had an instinct to retreat

from the intensity and find other things to do, other people to see, or to see no one at all.

Perhaps we should have stayed together. That is what friends are meant to do. And yet the sad fact was that we were simply better apart. I hoped we would run into one another someday soon. I didn't want to run away from them forever, because I knew I couldn't live without them forever. I knew I would run back soon. But for today—just one more distraction—one more train elsewhere.

And though it's easy to pretend the whole chase is merely a play of hedonism and carelessness, perhaps the more difficult truth is that, blasé and disaffected as our affectations are, we're looking for something more, still, though our attempts so often end in various shades of misery. Our attempts to know more result in hurting more. Our progressions eventually collapse our minds. Our passions tire us to faded silhouettes incapable of remembering what it was we yearned for in the beginning.

So I try to remember. What did happen?

How was the Wrecking Ball?

And in absence of a concrete reality I can grasp or remember—in the absence of a reality worth remembering—I write down stories, make-believe, fill in the gaps and lost hours . . . It might have all happened, I can't remember, can't know for sure.

Perhaps that is the freedom each of us yearned for in the beginning. Perhaps it is that looseness of being, that vagueness of reality, those clouds, that characterizes in a vague sketch the life we dreamt and realized, the freedom so impossible, and yet, so present in my dazed reminiscence.

And those things we would rather forget—the things that kicked us onto the road in the first place—the cause of our escape . . .

All that remains a hidden secret, obvious only in the painful throbbing of a bass line or the sad faint into the grass or faint tears nobody can see because you're wearing dark glasses and the sky is dark. You don't see the fuel in the lighter—only the fire. Sorrows drown before they make it into the conversation. We don't talk about the cause—only rebel against it, without it, at last, relishing the freedom from the memories we so despise.

The only fiction is the silence, the blank spaces on pages where certain confessions are not told. That is also part of the freedom. In silence the despair is put on mute, strangled to insignificance.

And yet silence has a habit of haunting one.

Still I believe we did with passion what we so desired to do—we chased that cloud, chased that dream, sang that song, felt the summer burn. We felt things deeply, we performed well. And after the morning and the hangover come and go, even after summer has faded out—still the songs remain—they play along, they play along forever. Eternity in an evening—every evening. Death each waking breath. My notebook and guitar stand in the corner, awaiting some life, giving me a reason to get up again and disturb the creeping silence, the invisible death, the passive smoke that would have me wilt and fade.

I play the songs and send the bad memories asunder.

I try to run away again, to somewhere better, for something higher.

ROSE

Drop beats not bombs, as they say, make love not war . . . Go to festivals not home . . . And if the glass is half empty—then it's time for a top-up.

The lawn stretches downhill where the crowds are gathering and the clouds are gone from the stretching skies. The lake glistens below. The gold wristbands shimmer in the light. I'm at Tales of the Jackalope at Pemberly Hall, Norfolk, with Bella, an amazing photographer who's wearing black leather shorts, a gold bag from Las Vegas and Blondie hair, and my little sister Clara . . . We're dazed and wandering, gazing and slumbering with the ease of the breeze and the soundtrack of something vaguely punk.

The afternoon passes in the same vein of sunny serenity and quickly it is evening and all the people have arrived. Including Michael Darcy, my new magazine editor, his girlfriend, another Clara, and a bunch of other people Bella knows from shoots and zines and bars and queens, obscene.

We drink rosé, move onto vodka, visit the purple tent, the blue tent, the red and yellow tent, talk to Michael and Clara and then go back to the beautiful house, to get a little to eat. We walk up the lawn, Pemberly radiant, a color somewhere in between rosé, peaches and cream. I have changed into a gold dress with a delicate pattern and dark patent platforms. Bella could have been Blondie. Clara wears coral. Michael has a new haircut. Someone says we look like a Testino shot. And we're not even posing on purpose.

Inside we are offered some soup, but prefer the wine because we're not really hungry. Someone tells me not to wear high heels at a festival because one day it will be the end of me but apparently cocaine is fine. The sun outside the window tints the room with warm light. The music from outside taints the silence with something toxic. And we want to hear more.

We drift back over the lawn and through the trees, where Michael asks,

"As the air is blowing slow, do we have a clean surface?"
. . . Yes, a little zine called *Vice*,
For a little bag of something nice.
(Cut it twice.)

We climb over a fence and wander down to the festival again, where we find a haystack to slumber on, telling stories and confessing confessions, as you do. In sync we all fall back, legs in the air, for a photograph by Bella. She shoots us down. And we like it.

Somewhere along the line and in the next few hours we listen to the Fall (we had a ball), the Rumble Strips and Lightspeed Champion . . . lyrical with a kind of passion like a sonnet, like a scrawled little love letter, lovers and clowns, ups and downs, voice and drums. Violin sent the lyrics airborne.

Us too. When high one tends to confess the things sobriety otherwise guards. We slumber on a haystack and Michael tells me about his girl and I tell him why my relationships keep ending before they ever really began. "All goes back to a night in November," I tell him, "I was faint from tiredness—really it was tiredness and nothing else—and missed the last train home—and four men picked me up and took me away out of the city and . . ."

I don't think he'll remember what I tell him come morning. I forget it myself minutes later, when some other band starts playing and the threatening silence disappears into a melody and we sniff a little more amnesia and forget what we would rather had never happened at all. The past disappears with the cocaine.

We take a little wander, then hang from railings by the stage, and Dizzee Rascal does his set, the crowds die of joy and we dance and smile a little while.

When it gets to about three a.m. we find ourselves in the Fucked Up gig, in the middle of a brawl, knocked down to the dirty old ground gazing up at fights and trysts and the big man smashing his head through something. Then the police turn up and take the mike and inform the restless mass that the show's over for whatever reason and with only a little protest the gig's fucked up but then that's what you'd expect I guess.

Bella and I go to the Dance Tent that is blue and dance for a while, but it's time for a drink or two and we sit on a haystack and watch or ignore the glamorous people walk by uber-stoned. The Diet Coke washes away the fatigue and numbs the cold breeze beginning to blow. Where is Michael?

Earlier in the day, albeit when the sun was shining down from the middle of the sky, we decided that we should all go midnight swimming and take photographs—drenched glamour, smeared mascara, bathing in debauchery au natural.

At four a.m. when it's cold and dark, it doesn't seem so bright an idea, but just the thought of escaping to the beautiful pool in a secret garden is enough to awaken our romantic visions and send us tripping through the dark wild woods in that vague direction.

Bella, Clara, a New Yorker from *Dazed & Confused* called Cindy, a Colombian girl with a great smile and a nose ring called Layla, some boy I never talked to, and another called Max, who nicked a blanket for us to use as a towel from someone's car, all jump in. I thought it would be freezing but it's actually pretty warm. The others think it's cold but I find it delicate and mellow and never want to leave. Someone is saying that "This is all so . . . spiritual . . ."

Max finds a little frog and we all kiss it and Bella takes a photo, perched on the side of the pool in some lingerie and that adorable platinum bob. Sadly the frog never turns into a prince.

We're all just innocently skinny-dipping when there's an unwanted entrance of two security guards. Did we invite them? No. No, no, no.

I start giggling and can't stop, and we're all laughing.

"Don't you want to join us?" I ask the younger one.

"No. I'm not allowed."

"We won't tell . . . Come on in, you know you want to . . ."

"You're not allowed in the pool," says the other security man.

"Yes, we are, we have special gold wristbands . . ." says Bella.

The security man says, "Do you all have gold wrist-bands?"

Little silence.

The sound of the water rippling and hushed laughter.

They talk to someone on their annoying little radio walkie-talkie thing. Then the security guard comes back and says that anyone not wearing a gold wristband has to leave pronto. I do have one so am happy to frolic around in the water for ages, especially as the sun has risen and the day looks so pretty and it doesn't feel cold at all.

But the others all get out. I continue swimming around. Max makes a big scene about having to get out and go back to the festival all cold and shivery. His pout is more pronounced than mine.

Bella, Cindy, Layla and the other guy are chilling on the swing chair. The security men are happy to watch everyone get out of the pool dripping, disheveled and scantily clad. Or not clad at all.

Eventually I'm told I have to stop swimming around and smoking cigarettes in the pool, otherwise I'll be left alone, all by myself, and we wouldn't want that because you can't have a party all by yourself.

So I get out and share the blanket Max nicked from someone's car (I think it was a tapestry or something, super soft) and try to persuade the security man that as we're sharing a towel, "Together—we have a wristband," but he says, "It doesn't work like that, darlin'."

The pool looks so good—Just one more time—I jump back in and swim around just a little more, it's amazing . . . Then when the others start to leave I climb out again a little forlorn that it all has to end.

Max gives me a piggyback through the woods and back to the Dance Tent, where we dance some more and then

Bella calls me and says there's a party in the house—Yay!—and I run off into the sunrise.

In the house the dumb security are being annoying about letting Rupert, a beautiful model, in without a wristband but we make it work. I can't go in looking like a Horror I realize so wipe some of the eyeliner from my face and skip in. We meet my older sister Skye and her husband Jamie (Pemberly is theirs), and meet their friends and chill and dry by the open fire with a gin and tonic. Then they go to a secret party on the roof and we stay downstairs and dance with the flames, and I remember much later about the "Feather Dance," which must have been embarrassing but it didn't feel that way at the time. I just remember dancing with two big red feathers to Blondie and all that other music for two hours as Rupert and Clara slumbered on the sofa in a little morning daze.

Bella miraculously finds a security walkie-talkie thing at this point, which leads to a few hours of prank calling the entire staff of security people. We feel the desire to get revenge on them for breaking up our little pool party.

We put on Yorkshire accents and say stuff like, "Alert! Alert! There—is—an—ORGY IN THE TEPEE! Closest to the lake. All security to the ORGY IN THE TEPEE immediately!"

Then, "Attention, Attention, someone in the Dance Tent has been spotted swallowing a pill. And something tells me it's not ibuprofen. All security to the Dance Tent."

Then we sing them some Blondie and something eighties and some Christina Aguilera.

Then we do "Confessions of a Tempted Security Man":

"Here I am, throwing people out and being an arse. But I feel restrained. To tell you the truth, I don't want to be throwing people out—I want to be throwing myself in. I want to be dropping the beats—not the law. I want to—I want to dance . . . That's that orgy I'm meant to be breaking up—but—I don't want to. And you know what? I'm not gonna. I'm going in—I'm going I—(ambiguous background noises) . . . Line breaks up . . ."

Then we listen to the real security people for a bit.

"Get off the fucking RADIO—You may find it funny, but I don't."

But we DO!

Then we hear someone say, "Alert! There is a fire in a tent"—seriously—so Bella says in her Yorkshire accent,

"Is it spreading?"

"No."

"Good, good."

Then we pretend we're doing Big Brother. Bella says, "It's seven forty-five a.m. in the Big Brother House. Nothing is happening. Some chickens are clucking, but nothing is happening."

Then we hear someone ask for cigarettes on the radio. So we say, "Yeah, me too, Emily. Marlboro Lights, I repeat, Marlboro Lights. Over and Out."

Then Bella starts choking on her gin from laughing and nearly dies because she stops breathing, because she has gin on the lungs.

It's very serious.

Then Jamie and the others (a music producer, an explorer and a photographer) come down wearing huge sunglasses and pretend they've been sleeping.

Some people drift in from breakfast at which point we drift back to our tepee. Actually we get driven there by an awesome music producer and we all chat in the tepee and

Rupert talks to him about hallucinogenics and it all gets a bit deep because Rupert's talking about how once, "I kept hearing a voice in my head. It kept saying, 'What the fuck are you doing? What are you doing?'—Then I realized it was my own voice."

Rupert and the Music Man leave soon after. Bella and Clara fall asleep. I wonder if I'm dreaming for a while about the pool and the security and the dancing and Dizzee and the moon and it all, but I haven't slept yet. The morning is mellow, and I lie back on my leopard-print mattress and sip water and notice the sky, a chink of which I can see at the top of the tepee, same color as the new bruises that color my legs, the blue Dance Tent and Clara's eyes, Michael's eyes, Skye's eyes, Bella's eyes, I remember, as I close my own.

ALICE

When I returned home from hospital I came back to a London coming down off of its summer high, a muggy breeze and the pretentious airs of passers-by. I was getting sick of Chelsea and Kensington, suddenly and for no real reason other than no one was there I wanted to see anymore, or who wanted to see me. They were all out of town or out of touch. I was out of sorts and out of vogue.

Quite the little rogue . . .

So I check into a hotel room because I can't think of anywhere else to go and I have a new credit card and I don't really have any money but I can pretend.

I take a bus to Chelsea again, I don't know why, perhaps to say good-bye to the shine of its vacuous wealth and blasé affectations and I get lost in an internal carousal of doubt, passion, delirium, depression, doubt. I listen to "Four Seasons in One Day" by Bob Dylan because every day has been that way the past year or two, and Hugo was that way, Harry that way too, and I'm tired of it. The carousal gets tedious after a while. Sloane Square, too. Shoreditch just the same. Where else is there to go in London? The park? Harvey Nichols? I have nothing to do but remember people who now forget me. Yet however much I'd like to move on I'm stuck on the pretty carousal, catching glances from people I keep seeing but don't know.

Then in a hotel room alone, hearing Harry's voice on an answer machine only, because I know it too, he'll never pick up. One line on repeat. How long must all this repeat? How many flashes of the bulb, how many shots, how many stupid fights, how many lonely nights, how many aimless walks through London all listless—all lustless. How many strangers on trains must I meet before I can find someplace to go, someone to know? Funny how boys just come—and go . . .

How many unrequited desires—canceled calls—broken falls—bathroom stalls . . . Must I trail before all this is more than lust for dust of dreams askew? How long before I leave? Run away after another shooting star . . .

ROSE

In the afternoon on Saturday, after Bella and I had arrived, pitched our tent, bought our cider—we frolicked through the hay, grass and mud finding our way to the music and glory.

We went and watched Joe Lean and the Jing Jang Jong and danced at the front and Bella kept making eye contact with the drummer, an old friend . . . The whole thing was blissful. There were a bunch of stoned fourteen-year-olds behind us doing some weird dance and it was shady inside the tent and cooler than the sunny mess outside.

After their set we sat down on the grass outside and smoked cigarettes with the band and took photos and went back to VIP for more cider and cigarettes, before a trip to see Babyshambles . . . I pushed into the center to hear a mesmerizing set, the crowds surrounding me in adoration, singing for a friendly grunge with rose petals scattered and sun beaming down on the scrum below. The sweat of strangers, the songs of experience . . . amorous and glamorous, down and out and dirty, with French girls and flags in the background . . .

Such was our desire to get a little closer, and lacking the elite passes required, Bella and I pretended we were from *NME* and *i-D* with an interview imminent, and were swiftly escorted backstage and given a pass for the Cider House backstage area which meant free drinks all weekend. We got some Bulmer's and then sneaked through an opening in the fence and sneaked through another backstage area, then another, eluding all the security guards, running over silver and grass . . .

I met Pete Doherty round the bands' trailers backstage and we talked for a moment amid the movement and flashes. He had a Union Jack draped over his left shoulder and beautiful eyes . . . such romantic and nonchalant poise, composure mixed with rebellious sublime. He wasn't even that wasted, seemed less so than Bella and me anyway.

"I sneaked all the way backstage just to see you," I told him.

"To see me?" He smiled back, his eyes glittering, his voice soft.

"Yeah."

"Thank you." He smiled in a teasing way and then someone caught his eye and he left with the band . . . walking slow but disappearing fast, something of a mirage blurring the atmosphere as he left.

I felt forlorn a little, standing round the trailers of the other bands, not wanting to see anyone else particularly, "What Katy Did" playing softly in my head.

Later we sneaked backstage—again without the security people noticing we didn't have the right pass or band or anything. Bella pretended to be Bobby Gillespie's wife and spun a whole story about babies and late nights and love. She pretended she was actually pregnant, and after much discussion with some official, decided on "Gigi Gillespie if it's a girl."

We managed to get up onto the stage itself and stood with Jarvis Cocker on the sidelines watching the gig, a triumph of energy and color, the mass of euphoric crowds cast in pink light. We danced and Jarvis Cocker was swigging red wine and then the Thrills turned up and we hung out with them. Halfway through Bella and I ran to another stage (ran all the way, and it was ages away) to see Bright Eyes, only to find, collapsed on something metal backstage, that they hadn't shown up. So we ran back to Primal Scream and despite the halfhearted lamentations of security, got back up on the stage again and watched the end of the set.

After that we left with the Thrills and drank champagne with them as we walked behind the stages, tour buses driving around slowly and security guards shining torches at us but nevertheless failing to catch us at all. We went back to the Thrills' trailer and then left for the VIP area where we drank Pimm's and ate noodles and talked and talked and talked: Literature and Dublin, Joyce and cigarettes, Love and War, Paris and London . . . After a bit we went back to their tour bus and hung out for a while with the guy from Jet as well, sleepy and happy. I lay down on some black cushions and we listened to music and talked some more to Connor and the roadie, Terry, mellow and dark outside.

I awoke to rain outside which was sad, and a random friend of someone in the Kooks the other side of the tent. Then I remembered how I hailed us a buggy that was luckily driving by the Thrills' tour bus and some friend of someone in the Kooks had no place to stay so we let him stay in our tent.

I went outside to wander and happened to meet a group of men from Brixton who were cooking breakfast and they said I could join then. They gave me bread and marijuana and we talked about the Cure.

I went back and Bella had woken up and the random boy had left. I'd been away some time. The rain laid off a bit so we went into the arena. We went to the backstage Cider House and got more free Bulmer's, then wandered into the main area. We were both really tired from our previous thrilling day so weren't going anywhere particularly fast. We saw a few more acts, then the Cribs, who were fun, playing the crowds with chutzpah and so much more wide awake than I was.

After that we went back to the VIP area and smoked cigarettes and found the cider wasn't having any effect anymore. We stayed until late afternoon before getting a call requesting our presence in London. Although we weren't too happy about missing Kasabian in particular, it was obvious that Saturday was better than Sunday. I was so mesmerized by all that had happened and all we had heard that we didn't need to stick around in the mud much longer. We beat the crowds and left a bit early. Never be the last to leave the party, as they say. We picked the Hawley for a post-V pit stop.

It was still raining and felt like November rather than August, all dark at midnight, the wind was blustering rough, we smoked outside where the lighting was amber, I played with the bands on my wrist and talked to people and got a bit wet . . . Crowds dispersed and we wandered off and disappeared from the last festival of the summer, charmed and changed, in love and deranged, unable to stand the thought of another nine months or so before another festival awakens me from a quotidian slumber again—again, just do it again.

ALICE

And gazing at the view out the window, the sun setting again, the summer drawing to a dusky close . . . I gaze into the sky intently, alone once more, coming down from the blaze of summer, the haze of Harry, with no energy left, only the serenity of a sunset absorbing my mind. Lines of plays to learn.

Pink and gold painted over dusky cornflower blue, distance colored lazy angelic yellow, pale and deep at once, shades of smoggy gray touched with smudges and sparks of azure—floating sublime, sparks together like a flock of birds. Gold turns to scarlet with a crest of brushed dark purple. Streaks of pink and navy blue decorated the distance. An island in the sky—vacuous, intoxicating and drenched with allure—darts of neon orange hitting the dirty baby blue twilight. The train is moving past silver pools and streams, fragile branches of darkened trees, darts of crimson, shadowed fields, flooded fields reflecting steel and pearly gray. Violet brushstrokes are smudging up the sky with natural elation and mystique—fluorescent streaks . . . Then a large indigo mass of cloud drags the blue sky further in, sweeps it in with irresistible night. The darts and streaks of gold and lit azure disappear like islands sinking and shooting stars fading. Pushed low into the gravity of the earth's horizon, quickly the blue expanse disappears, and only this darkened indigo night remains, the vibrancy now gone into quietude and slumber, the twilight ended, the play begun.

HARRY

Gray clouds like cigarette smoke fade with the night as Manhattan is illuminated by the early morning, lines of dark red mixed with charcoal, painted over pale green and amber and blue, deepening with height, a few tiny white stars glittering, strewn across the dawn. Just got back into town, sitting in Central Park with coffee.

I am starting to write songs again. I can feel them playing under my skin, echoing in my mind, that sort of feeling where I'll go crazy if I don't write them down soon. It excites me, I feel alive once more. And the drugs are slowly disappearing from my desires. I have been feeling dizzy for a few days and sick from the withdrawal, have been feeling a bit out of it, but the general clarity with which I hear life is surprisingly immediate and gives me a new sort of high: a creative high, a clean breath, a new start.

Where towers fell,
Where grandeur fell to dust,

Where money turned to ash,
Where dreams were sold for hash
Love was lost to lust
My mind became my hell

I can only rebel.

As night falls into the ocean, dawn breaks the darkness to pieces, invisible between rays of sun, melting into oblivion. The wrecking ball is a sort of sun, the morning after . . .

A violet haze smudged across a bright yellow sunrise, clear blue morning. Thick mist—blue, gray, smothering trees, lawns and darkened towers . . . Then diffusing to reveal gold, birds heading west across an indigo skyline and crimson mist. Clouds the color of faded summer roses smeared across the dawn and electric cyan height, purple dust out east, gold streaks picking up pale yellow edge:

The fringe of day, the edge of light.

ACKNOWLEDGMENTS

With thanks to Carrie Kania, Brittany Hamblin, and everyone else at Harper Perennial.

Also thank you to Simon Petherick, Tamsin Griffiths, Kathryn Josselyn, Jenny Stanley-Clark and everyone at Beautiful Books in London—and to Christopher Rush for introducing us.

My parents, Michael and Janet Spens, have been brilliant parents and writers, and have taught me through experience to live passionately and courageously. And to my beautiful sisters Flora and Mariota.

Thank you to my older sister Iona and her husband Robbie for teaching me about cocktails, flying and fun. . . And to my godparents Jutta and Wolfgang Fischer, Barbie Kane and Nick Waterlow for their love and encouragement.

I would have got bored of London a long time ago (and never written this novel) were it not for the friendship and generosity of my wonderful friends, especially Tom Hannan, Matt Ingram, Alex Pyper, David Spens, Nick Howard,

Bella Howard, Michelle Chaso and Sebastian Horsley. My love also to old and new friends at home and elsewhere, especially Natalie Jones, Dora Somerville, Tess Brokaw, and Adela Crone, who has read everything I have ever written, knows every single secret and can read between the lines like no other.

About the author

About the book

Read on

Insights,
Interviews
& More . . .

Meet Christiana Spens

Mariota Spens

CHRISTIANA SPENS is a student at the University of Cambridge in England. Born in Melbourne, Australia, Christiana has lived in Scotland, London, New York, and Tennessee. She enjoys ballet and painting, and has written art and fashion pieces for *Studio International* since she was fifteen years old, and continues to write for Rockfeedback.com. This is her first novel. ∼

A Conversation with Christiana Spens

So I can't help but notice from your photo, you seem to be on the young side. When did you start writing?

I've been writing since I can remember, but I think it became more serious when I was about sixteen. It always felt like a natural thing to do. I wrote the novel when I was nineteen, in about three weeks, but it was the culmination of about two years' work.

Describe your childhood.

I grew up mostly in Scotland, near the sea, as well as in London and Sydney. I have two younger sisters and we had a creative, mostly happy childhood. We traveled a lot and I was restless from a young age. I loved dancing and painting and music. In hindsight it was quite a bohemian upbringing.

Did you enjoy school? Were you the bookworm type or a social butterfly?

I didn't particularly like school. I did well in classes, but I always didn't like being told what to do all the time. As I got older I'd bunk off with my best friend Adela, we'd go down to the beach and coffee shops and smoke and plan our escape. I lived in a daydream.

You've lived all over the world—what cities inspire you, which do you detest, where are the best spots to write? ▶

> ❝ I wrote the novel when I was nineteen, in about three weeks, but it was the culmination of about two years' work. ❞

My sister (right) and I at a toga party in Cambridge.

A Conversation with Christiana Spens
(continued)

I don't think there's any place I detest—though there are parts of London I'm not that keen on, basically anywhere beyond Zone 2 I wouldn't bother with. My favorite cities are Paris, New York, and New Orleans, and of course I love London too. I haven't been back to Sydney in ages, though I remember feeling really free and happy there. I think I feel inspired anywhere I feel free.

I've always felt that I feel more at home in Paris than London for some reason, it's just a bit more beautiful and sensuous. It doesn't feel real, it's like the whole place is drenched in illusion. The galleries there are wonderful, and the coffee is the best. I'd say the best place to write is probably La Closerie de Lilas. Apparently Hemingway wrote *The Sun Also Rises* there, so I'm in good company. I got caught in the rain one day and rushed into the restaurant, and the coffee was so good (and the rain so heavy) I stayed three hours. The waiter kept bringing me more coffee and cake on the house, and I started writing a passage that I ended up using in my novel a couple years later.

Also I would recommend Café Flore. I like this place not only because the coffee is good but because it sounds like my sister Flora, whom I missed at the time. But there are so many good cafés in Paris and I forget most of the names . . . I still have a lot of exploring to do.

For me, the places I found in London to be good for writing were:

The Lansdowne Club is where I edited my novel during the summer when my laptop broke. It has lots of pretty rooms and a business center, and a pool, which is refreshing after writing for hours. Also their drinks menu is really good, which obviously helps.

66 The waiter [at La Closerie de Lilas] kept bringing me more coffee and cake on the house, and I started writing a passage that I ended up using in my novel a couple years later. 99

Green Park: When it's sunny it's a nice place to relax, and I went there a lot in the summer as it's also near the Lansdowne.

Soho Square: one of the few places in London where people smoke weed and don't get caught. Having said that, in recent months the police have started hanging around there and my friends and I got lifted for drinking Pimm's at nine p.m. It was all a bit embarrassing really and we had to find a little alley to drink the rest of our stash, like we were criminals or something.

The French House, on Dean Street, is always stimulating. Fun people go there. It's also where we have publishing meetings sometimes.

Also I was recently taken to the Colony Rooms by Sebastian Horsley and I loved it there. I felt like I'd been there before. I swear I was someone's muse in a past life. The 1920s probably. They probably didn't let women in the Colony Rooms back then, but I would have found a way.

What is the oddest job you've ever had? Anything memorably dangerous, bizarre, notably mundane?

When I was in high school in Memphis, just after graduation and the Beale Street Music Festival, I met this film director in Starbucks. I suddenly had this intense feeling that I had to talk to him, and we got on and he offered me a job as a runner on his crime film. I went to a small town in Tennessee and it was the most bizarre experience. The story was about this transvestite nanny who abducted two kids, then got caught, and only then was it discovered she was a transvestite. It was June and burning hot outside, and I had all these weird jobs like drawing fake tattoos on the ▶

> ❝ I met this film director in Starbucks. I suddenly had this intense feeling that I had to talk to him, and we got on and he offered me a job as a runner on his crime film. ❞

A Conversation with Christiana Spens
(continued)

redneck dad, lying in a ditch by the Mississippi for four hours with a smoke machine, and dressing up as the trashy mother at one point as the actress's double. It was really fun.

You mentioned you've studied acting—what would your ideal role be?

Marie Antoinette, perhaps.

Would you ever work on a soap opera?

Never!

Everyone knows the candy is better in the UK. What's your favorite sweet?

Dark chocolate with chili extract.

How does music factor into your writing?

I think music probably influences me as much as literature. I love lots of bands— Primal Scream, the Libertines, the Strokes, White Stripes, Air, Sonic Youth . . . I could go on forever. And I love different festivals in different ways. Latitude last year was really laid back and relaxing, V Festival was exciting because we were backstage the whole time and it was so big . . . I'm not really that picky. Any excuse to lie around in the sunshine with bands, really.

> ❝ I'm not really that picky. Any excuse to lie around in the sunshine with bands, really. ❞

You're trapped in a mountain lodge during an avalanche with your dog Max (humor me). What books, films, CDs keep you sane while you wait for help?

Anything by Fitzgerald, Hemingway, Kerouac, Colette, McInerney, and Ellis . . . And films—*Marie Antoinette, Almost Famous, Pulp Fiction, Breakfast at Tiffany's, Lost in Translation, Brokeback Mountain, The*

Secretary, and *Leon* . . . And lots of records, wine, and magazines.

Alice and Rose have a passion for clothing—is this your scene? Who are your favorite designers?

Yeah, I drift in and out of that scene. I love Vivienne Westwood, Chanel, and Armani most of all. Also I like the early illustrations Andy Warhol did for *Vogue* and beautiful fashion photography. It is all pretty frivolous but a lot of work goes into couture, and that sort of perfectionist work ethic is something I admire.

Anything you've drawn or painted or photographed that you'd like to show? ▶

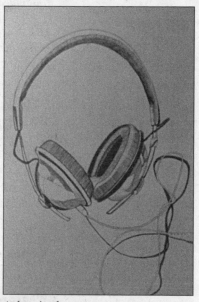

A drawing by me.

A photograph of the band the Bloody Social.

A Conversation with Christiana Spens
(continued)

Drink of choice? And are you even old enough to drink?

Well, technically not in America . . . Basically I like Pimm's and martinis, Jack Daniel's and Coke. I like trying new things.

What does your family think about the book?

My sister loves it. She's my age and it's perfect for her. My parents are proud of me. I keep having to remind them it's fictional. Not that many other people have read it. I'm trying to avoid elderly relatives reading it. No one believes me when I say all the criminal stuff is fictional.

Any notable romances?

I'm not telling.

What are you reading now?

I just finished reading Sebastian Horsley's *Dandy in the Underworld*, which was really funny. We went to the Borders in Soho and he bought it for me, while I rearranged the bestsellers list in his favor. Also I'm reading *The Unmade Bed* by Françoise Sagan and *Rock 'n' Roll* by Tom Stoppard.

What's the best class you've taken?

Ballet class with this ex-Bolshoi soloist called Dmitri Roudnev, at the Hutchison School in Memphis.

What must you do before you die?

Love, party, dance . . .

> 66 I just finished reading Sebastian Horsley's *Dandy in the Underworld*, which was really funny. We went to the Borders in Soho and he bought it for me, while I rearranged the bestsellers list in his favor. 99

On Writing
The Wrecking Ball

Golden Insomnia

I wrote *The Wrecking Ball* when I was nineteen, in between finishing high school in Memphis and starting Cambridge. I took a year out and lived in London, but I ran out of money and energy and the will to go on halfway through the year. At that point I left London, went back home to Scotland and attempted to sort myself out. I hung out with my old friends from home—we shared stories and smoked and drank too much and helped each other through the freezing winter. The smoking ban had unfortunately just come through so we sat in the outside areas of bars in St. Andrews drinking cocktails and chain-smoking our troubles away.

I had been writing a lot, absentmindedly almost, the whole time I had been living in London and America and flitting from place to place, but my previous writing lacked focus. So in February I gave myself four weeks to write a new novel. I happened to be insomniac at the time, which probably helped, and I had a draft done in three weeks. By May I had a publisher, Beautiful Books, and the contract with Harper Perennial followed. I redrafted the novel over the summer, in between going to festivals and parties and interning at a music company in Soho.

Writing the novel was an attempt to give the chaos some order, to give the wrecking ball a tangible end.

I wrote the novel because, when all else had become impossible, writing was the reflex. It was all I wanted to do—the only true escape when every other exit was cut off. ▶

> ❝ Writing the novel was an attempt to give the chaos some order, to give the wrecking ball a tangible end. ❞

A Roman à Clef?

Before I wrote *The Wrecking Ball* I wrote an autobiographical novel, when I was traveling in Paris and America. However, I felt it lacked something—I'd written the details but the essence of the experience was missing. It didn't have much plot or direction, I didn't know what or why I was writing, I simply wrote because it felt like a natural thing to do.

When I then wrote *The Wrecking Ball* I had a better concept of the novel as a story detached from my own life. Although some of my own experiences inevitably seeped into the finished novel, to begin with I wanted to write something that conveyed a bigger picture, not only about my own life but just everything I'd seen and heard. I wanted it to be satirical and light. The three years that led up to writing the novel had been incredibly dramatic and temperamental; in writing the novel I wanted to contain that energy as well as break away from it. I can see why people would assume the novel to be quite autobiographical, but in fact when writing the novel I felt as though I had to escape and forget myself in order to truly inhabit the fictional characters. I had to think very abstractly when I was writing. Details of my life became mere material with which to illustrate scenes. In that sense writing is more like method acting, you use whatever history you have to fulfill the role. Of course some of the passages in the novel are similar to my own life, but that's beside the point. As a writer I have quite a fluid sense of self anyway. I'm curious about other people, curious about changing and escaping and different sensations. The characters in the novel are flights, they're connected to me but they're ultimately separate entities.

> 66 Although some of my own experiences inevitably seeped into the finished novel, to begin with I wanted to write something that conveyed a bigger picture, not only about my own life but just everything I'd seen and heard. I wanted it to be satirical and light. 99

I'm no more one major character than another. I don't see my friends in the characters either, but the dynamics of relationships I have had are definitely present in the novel. Strangely, since writing the novel, I have met people who seem very similar to the fictional characters, which is slightly bizarre. Sometimes the patterns in life are far stranger than fiction, and sometimes they simply run parallel.

The Hardest Scene
I found the ending most difficult. It was hard to let go, hard to find an ending I was happy with, but that was also true to the characters and novel as a whole. Also the passages where the characters are in the midst of breakdown and addiction were draining. When I was actually writing them I was so involved it didn't feel particularly difficult, just rather distressing. But after writing I felt exhausted and a little confused. It's hard to distinguish between emotional fact and fiction sometimes. It's hard to reconcile with reality after being so involved in a fictional scenario.

Odds and Obstinacy:
The Path to Publication
The first person I talked to was an editor at Canongate, and he was really supportive and encouraging about the process and about being persistent, and that gave me a positive outlook from the beginning. Otherwise the publishing industry seemed daunting and endless. I tried not to think of rejection too much, I just got on with it. After writing the novel, getting a publisher was relatively simple. Sending out letters was refreshingly banal after all the emotional exhaustion of writing *The Wrecking Ball*. ▶

I wanted someone to take the book so that I could have a break from it. I wanted it to be over, and had this idea that if some editor picked it up I would be able to let it go and get on with my life. I've since learned that it isn't quite that simple. I have now surrendered to being a writer—whether I'm published or not, writing will probably always take over my life whether I like it or not. It's just a matter of embracing it not fighting it.

In hindsight the odds were against me, and I was very lucky. I was rejected by a few agents but one gave me some really good advice, so it felt like I was making progress. Then I talked to a neighbor in Scotland, Chris Rush, who had just signed with Beautiful Books, a new independent publisher, and he suggested I try them. A few weeks later I had a contract. And then a few months later Carrie Kania, at Harper Perennial, picked it up at the Frankfurt Book Fair. This was incredibly lucky and I'm so grateful!

Influences

Three stories had a specific influence on *The Wrecking Ball*: *Alice in Wonderland*, *The Beautiful and Damned* and *Hamlet*. These are stories that I'd read awhile back but that always resonated with me, and the themes in each seemed to correspond in an abstract way.

In a general sense, I was influenced a lot by Symbolist poetry and art, and the Surrealist movement. Edgar Allan Poe, Rimbaud and Baudelaire definitely inspire me. I have always connected literature with art and music, so instances when these entwine—for example, Blake's work— particularly interest me. I always had an

66 I have now surrendered to being a writer—whether I'm published or not, writing will probably always take over my life whether I like it or not. 99

affinity for the Romantic poets—Byron and Tennyson especially—also Flaubert's *Madame Bovary* and *A Sentimental Education*. I went through a phase when I was about fourteen of reading lots of philosophy—Camus, Sartre, Nietzsche, et cetera. I was going through an existential crisis or something. Nothing bad had even happened when I was fourteen . . .

I read a lot of plays—Shakespeare, Chekhov, Tennessee Williams, Mamet, Miller and screenplays. I wrote plays before I wrote prose, in fact. I prefer the structure of plays to novels generally.

I didn't read much English literature until after I came back from America, and then it was mostly just Oscar Wilde and Martin Amis. When I was growing up I read mostly American and French novels. I liked reading Fitzgerald, Hemingway, McInerney, Plath, Hunter S. Thompson, Bret Easton Ellis . . . also Colette and Jean Cocteau's *Les Enfants Terribles* and Anaïs Nin. I'm reading some Will Self now.

Joyce had a major influence on me; *Portrait of the Artist as a Young Man* was definitely a turning point. The other two most influential books for me were Tolstoy's *Anna Karenina* and Fitzgerald's *Great Gatsby*. They were so sublime. ∽

> 66 I didn't read much English literature until after I came back from America, and then it was mostly just Oscar Wilde and Martin Amis. 99

Author's Picks
Finding Trouble in New York and London

New York

What is it about New York that draws you in?

I don't really know what draws me to
New York—it just glimmers and glitters
like no place else. It's a bit like London,
but it's more new and exciting, and the
whole city has a heightened energy I adore.
Everything I love is there—and a sense of
unreality. It seems lawless and yet controlled.
And I always meet fun people whenever I go.

Perhaps if I actually lived there it would
lose its novelty though. Some photographer
once told me that if you love anyone or
anything you shouldn't see them too often
because it will kill the romance. New York
is always a bit of a fling for me. And yet
I keep going back for more . . .

- *Best posh bite to eat:* The Waverly Inn.
  My friend Tess and I first went there after
  Beatrice banned us (for about two days).
  (We were going to spend Christmas
  there and everything.) We went in and
  one of the co-owners was so sweet, she
  bought us drinks and told us we were
  beautiful. Unfortunately, she then
  suggested we all go to Beatrice together.
  We tried to explain that maybe this
  wasn't a great idea but she dragged us
  along anyway. It wasn't pretty.

  However, fate had now introduced us
  to the Waverly and we went back again
  and again.

- *Best dive bar:* I can never remember the
  names . . .

- *Best club:* We have now forgiven Beatrice.

- *Best dark corner to make out in:* Basement of Don Hill's.

- *Best deals on clothes:* Everywhere, considering the current exchange rate.

- *Best neighborhoods:* Tribeca and the East Village.

London

And what about London draws you in?

I have a bit of a love-hate relationship with London. Although most of my favorite people live in London, the city as a whole can get a bit tedious if you hang around too long. I feel bad saying that though. Out of everywhere in the UK, London is definitely my favorite place. It manages to be dirty and elegant simultaneously, and a lot of the people are like that too. The music scene is the best; I feel completely happy and at home when I'm seeing a friend's band play or something. That side of London I adore. But then there's a vacuous boring commercial side that isn't chic at all; it's dull. I think New York is better at being glamorous, there's more of a rush and it's more playful. London, however, has an inimitable sense of style, an integrity, that I will always love and respect.

- *Best posh bite to eat:* The Wolsely is the best. They have lots of good traditional food and it's spacious and chic, but always bustling with people. It's not pretentious at all, just welcoming. It's perfect for brunch. I like the black and white floor.

- *Best dive bar:* The Toucan bar off Soho Square has a cute basement and I like going there. The best place ever used to be Push Bar in Soho, but, tragically, it ▶

Author's Picks *(continued)*

shut down. The Hawley Arms was great
but it just burned down.

• *Best club:* At the moment, Punk in Soho
on Thursdays. There are lots of places; it's
good to be spontaneous and go to
different places all the time. Shoreditch
House is quite happening right now.
Bungalow 8 is totally overrated.

• *Best dark corner to make out in:* Soho
is a dark corner to make out in.

• *Best deals on clothes:* You can find
interesting things in vintage stores
round the King's Road and also
Camden.

• *Best neighborhood:* For music,
Camden; I love Chelsea as well,
it's green and pretty. ❧

D**on't miss the next
book by your favorite
author. Sign up now for
AuthorTracker by visiting
www.AuthorTracker.com.**